CW00863052

Island of ⅃ℎe Ghost Bear

B.J. JOHNSON
TIM SWOPE ILLUSTRATOR

ISLAND OF THE GHOST BEAR

A NOVEL

Imprint Books

2003

To Jenny,
Enjoy!
B) John

Island of the Ghost Bear

To Jessyn and Ben

PROLOGUE

Grandfather's stories always made me feel like I was there—there when Raven turned the black bear white. When Grandfather told me how it was, I could see Raven flying over an island where no humans ever walked. I watched him diving deep into the forest, flying low between the mammoth cedars. I heard the beating of his wings as he dipped down over a sleeping black bear, touching him lightly with his talons and turning him a pure white. And when he was finished patrolling the island, having turned every tenth bear white, Raven's call echoed into the forest. "Peace!" he cried. The Island of the Ghost Bear was to be at peace forever.

1
Eagle

Daniel sat on a sidewalk in downtown Seattle, concentrating on the cedar plank in his lap. With each whittle of the wood, he was turning the board into Ghost Bear being touched by Raven. But he had to work fast because he needed the cash. He had told Grandfather he would call his older brother, Leonard, as soon as he got to the City, but it had been weeks, and he hadn't done that yet. Grandfather would be worried. He recalled the hopeful look on Grandfather's face as the small old Indian man watched the ferry pull away from the dock on Hannah Island in Alaska, taking his grandson south to Seattle.

I just need to make enough money on my carvings and Leonard will let me stay in Seattle, Daniel thought. Yes, maybe tonight he'd call.

A blast of diesel exhaust made Daniel stop digging his little carving knife into the cedar wood and look up. A busload of tourists was about to disembark. His carving might catch their attention. Sure enough, a young woman got off the bus and headed toward his little sidewalk encampment.

"Excuse me, what are you carving?" she inquired.

Daniel brushed his shaggy black hair out of his eyes and looked directly up at the lady—making eye contact was something he had learned worked with tourists. "My grandfather showed me how to make the cuts just right so that Raven wouldn't play a nasty trick on me. This is a raven and a bear. Whadda ya think of it? Will I get tricked or will you buy my carving?"

"How much is it?" the lady responded with a little smile.

"Seventy five dollars. Check out the eagle I carved yesterday."

As the woman examined the carving, Daniel fingered the frayed neck of his tee shirt and wondered if the woman would think he was a just a street kid. As soon as he sold some more carvings, he repeated to himself, he'd call Leonard.

"I'll take the one you're working on," she said, as her companions approached. "It would look lovely on my living room wall."

Daniel could almost hear Raven cackling. He promised that he'd have it finished by the time she got settled in the hotel and came out for some sightseeing. Of course, he would. In the two weeks that he had been in the City, he'd gotten used to working as fast as was necessary, even if the cuts weren't as perfect, "deep carved," as his Grandfather—or Raven—thought they should be. He would use shoe polish instead of fish oil to make it shine and rub it with just as many strokes as time permitted. But the tourist lady would be

3

pleased, and maybe buy some carvings. Then he would go to Pioneer Square and hang out with his friends.

As Daniel headed toward Pioneer Square, a hundred and twenty five dollars in his pocket—the lady couldn't resist the eagle carving either—he thought about the bald eagles he had seen that morning along the waterfront. Two baby eagles sitting in the tallest fir tree looking down into the water. Though they were huge compared to the crow twitting about them, he could tell by their mottled brown coloring and their fluffy dark heads that they were young. No one he passed—not the joggers or the homeless men—seemed to notice the birds. No one seemed to hear the staccato "Scree-ee-ee!" of the eagle mother hurrying back to her young. Her white head swiveled back and forth and her eye caught his. He knew she was worried that he had taken notice of her brood.

"Danny, when an eagle stares you in the eye, that's somethin'. Things are gonna change," he remembered Grandfather saying on their walks along the beach, back home on Hannah Island.

Yes, he thought, this must be a sign that he would make some good money. And now, with two carvings sold, he was sure of it.

I'll call Leonard tonight, he thought as he walked along. Touching the bulging cash in his pocket, he started sprinting down the street, with a burst of energy his adolescent body couldn't contain.

The sound of sirens, as commonplace in the city as the sound of ravens in the country, was something Daniel didn't register at all. Then, out of the corner of his eye, he saw a car stop and two policemen jump out. As he ran, he suddenly realized that the two were running after him.

His legs shot him ahead faster; his feet felt as if they were barely touching the ground.

No thought of why, no thought of anything but the chase. Just outrun them and find a place to hide.

He could hear their even steps behind him and almost feel their breath, and then they started lagging behind. Just as he was about to dart into an alleyway, another car came careening down the street ahead of him. The car jerked to a stop and a policeman jumped out, running toward him. Figuring he wouldn't make it to the alleyway, he dashed into the busy street. He dodged an oncoming car and hurdled a newspaper stand on the other side of the street. He turned into what he hoped was a passageway between the two buildings. The steps behind him echoed between the brick walls and became fainter and fainter as he ran.

He was beating them.

Then he spotted the dead end.

He knew he was caught.

The policemen converged on Daniel. Breathless, heart pounding out of his chest, Daniel fell to the ground. As they grabbed his arms, the short, squat cop noted the tips of the twenty-dollar bills in his pocket.

"Yeah, this is one of 'um. Check out the wad of cash in his pocket. The other two Indian kids must be ahead of him."

They pulled Daniel to his feet and made him put his hands against the cold, clammy brick wall as high as he could reach. The tall cop frisked him. Daniel felt humiliated.

"Right. Look at this," the cop said, holding up the small carving knife he had pulled out of Daniel's other jeans pocket.

Walking back down the alley, his arms gripped tightly by both policemen, gave Daniel a chance to absorb the magnitude of what had happened to him. Were they taking him to jail?

Why hadn't he called Leonard sooner? Why did he even think he could impress Leonard? Is this what the eagle's eye meant?

* * *

In the juvenile detention center, Daniel stood at the booking desk between the same two policemen. A clerk sitting across from them asked him his birth date. At Daniel's response, one of the policemen said, "Not even 13? What are you doing on the streets? Where's your family?"

Instead of answering, Daniel's mind raced. *Should I tell him I sold a carving? That I wanted to make some money before I got in touch with my brother?*

He won't believe me, he decided.

Finally he mumbled, "Alaska. My brother is Leonard Martin." And then, as he was about to dig in his pocket for the paper his grandfather had carefully written his brother's number on, he recalled being frisked and paused. Instead he said, "His number's in my pocket."

The policeman replied, "Go ahead, give it to me."

Finding the crumpled piece of paper he thought, *What will Leonard think when he sees me here?*

An image of Leonard returning home, coming through the door of their doublewide after their mother died, flashed through his mind. Then he pictured Leonard announcing that he had to leave. He said he had this great opportunity—an important commission—to work on with Charlie Amber in Seattle. But if Leonard hadn't left, none of this would have happened!

"Call this kid's brother," the tall policeman said, handing the clerk the number.

Then Daniel was led into a cell already occupied by two older teens. These must be the two they said were running ahead of him, Daniel guessed. They must be the ones that actually robbed the convenience store.

He sat down on the bench across the cell from them and joined them in staring at the floor. Would these two tell the police that they had never seen Daniel before? He doubted it. Would he try to explain himself? He doubted that too. The two cops who caught him had already made it clear they thought he was guilty.

The voices in the police station faded and Daniel's mind drifted back to his home. He could hear the villagers talking. "Leonard...only 16 when he became an apprentice of that famous artist, Charlie Amber. ...Leonard went to college, traveled to Europe, a totem pole of Leonard's stands outside a museum."

Now, Daniel thought, *they're calling Leonard and telling him I'm a thief!*

When he heard Leonard's voice coming from the front desk, his first reaction was relief. But then, when he thought of what Leonard must be thinking, a wave of shame washed over him. Leonard was telling the police that Daniel had just come to the City from Hannah island in Alaska, where he lived with their grandfather since both parents were dead, father killed years ago in a logging accident and mother dying of tuberculosis just a few years ago.

"—first time in trouble. ...Maybe got in with the wrong crowd."

Then Leonard suggested the boy would give the money back, and he would take his younger brother into his own custody until he delivered him back to his grandfather. Leonard sounded business-like talking to the police, even though he was only 26. When Daniel saw him approaching the cell accompanied by a guard, he looked like the successful artist that he was, his jet-black hair smoothed back into a neat ponytail, bright white linen shirt, leather shoes, beige cargo pants.

When they opened the cell to let Leonard take him away, Daniel couldn't look his brother in the eyes. He just followed him through the detention center and kept the ground fixed under his stare.

Daniel brooded. Did Leonard actually believe the police? Maybe he did. After all, Leonard had left him for his "important commission"—what does Leonard know about him now?

Outside, Leonard put his arm around his younger brother and steered him down the street. When they came to a park bench, Leonard suggested they stop and decide where to go from there. As they sat down, the only thing Daniel took in was a picture on the front page of a newspaper in the stand next to the bench. It was a picture of a young woman sitting atop a tree with a logger below, pointing a chainsaw up at her. The caption was "Young woman saves tree from logging."

Then Daniel continued to concentrate on the ground, until the ruckus on a garbage can nearby couldn't be ignored. A crow had dropped a candy bar onto the lid and every crow in the neighborhood gathered round to bicker over it.

Leonard asked, "Are you hungry, Danny? Let's get some grub and you can tell me about Grandfather."

* * *

Leonard's apartment smelled of cedar wood and oil but soon Daniel was aware of only eggs and bacon sizzling in a pan. They sat down at Leonard's kitchen table and began downing big plates of food.

Leonard slid another couple of fried eggs on Daniel's plate

and asked, "Grandfather and Uncle Henry do a lot of fishin' this Spring?"

Daniel was relieved that his brother hadn't asked what happened earlier that day, but it pained him now to think about Grandfather. How disappointed Grandfather would be if he knew about the mess Daniel had gotten into! He forced himself to answer. "Fishin' wasn't so good. Uncle Henry says the salmon runs get worse every year."

"That's what I've heard. Leaves Uncle Henry too much time on his hands, I'm afraid. I suppose he spends it in the tavern," Leonard said, looking disappointed. "How about rockfish?"

"Small. Grandfather says people are catching too many fish, and the fish aren't getting old enough. You gotta go up north now to catch the big ones. Grandfather might not even bother going out next year."

Leonard didn't reply and stopped eating. It made Daniel nervous. Would Leonard now ask him how long he had been in Seattle—and would Daniel tell him the truth if he did? Then Daniel's attention was drawn to a wooden mask hanging on the wall. It was a beautiful black and red carved eagle.

"That mask was carved maybe by an ancestor of ours. There aren't too many masks like that around." Leonard said. Daniel was startled that his brother had followed his gaze.

"Say, Danny," Leonard continued, "you know Grandfather's story of Great-Great Grandfather's wedding?"

Good, Daniel thought. *A story.* It didn't matter that Daniel had heard this story over and over ever since he was a small boy. *No questions for a while.* He nodded yes, knowing that Leonard would tell the story anyway.

"So remember how Grandfather told us about Great-Great Grandfather and his family? They sailed for days in a fifty-foot canoe with a sail woven from cedar bark and sea serpents carved on the sides? They sailed to a large island where Great-Great Grandfather was to meet his bride. When they came close to shore, he put on an incredible eagle mask carved out of cedar and a woven robe trimmed with feathers and jumped up on a plank that they had placed across the gunwales."

Daniel put his fork down and listened intently. Listening was, thankfully, letting him forget about what had happened that day.

"As they paddled in to shore, Great-Great Grandfather danced on the platform and waved his arms up and down as if he would take off. The rest of the family chanted and sang, some paddling while the others beat on painted skin drums. From the shore, Great-Great Grandfather must have really looked like an eagle, flapping his wings. Great-Great Grandmother's family was really impressed at the sight of them. And her father held a potlatch—a ceremony and a feast—that was the biggest anyone could remember.

"Did Grandfather ever tell you what happened to Great-Great Grandfather at the potlatch?"

Daniel shook his head no. The part about the canoe trip was all that he could remember of Grandfather's story.

"He was in the center of the big house, dancing all alone around the fire. Everyone was in full regalia sitting on the platform surrounding the fire in the center. They were all watching him. Anyway, he was wearing his huge eagle mask and dancing to a drumbeat—really getting into it, thinking he was impressing Great-Great Grandmother's family. Then all of a sudden everyone, especially Great-Great Grandmother, burst out laughing."

"Why?" Daniel asked, wondering how he had somehow missed this part of the story.

"Well," Leonard said, "there was Great-Great Grandfather dancing around the fire, when his deerskin dance tunic fell off! He was the only one not to notice. So until he realized why everyone was laughing, he kept on dancing with his bare bottom blazing in the fire light."

Leonard went on with his story. "The wedding celebration lasted for three days. Great-Great Grandmother's father gave everyone gifts and they all danced and told stories and ate the whole time. Great-Great Grandfather's dances and stories came from his clan—the Eagle clan. Great-Great Grandmother's side was the Raven clan. But all the children kept mimicking Great-Great Grandfather's dance, then giggling. They thought Raven was up to his old tricks loosening the strings on his tunic.

"But," Leonard concluded, "I think Great-Great Grandmother's brothers had a hand in it."

* * *

That night, curled up on the sofa, Daniel kept seeing himself running through the streets of Seattle. He pictured himself standing at the booking desk in the juvenile detention center. He pictured Leonard talking to the two policemen. Again he wondered if Leonard actually believed he was a robber. It felt like they didn't even know each other anymore. Then his mind flipped to the story about their great-great grandparents' wedding, and something occurred to him. Maybe Leonard had made part of the story up—the part about Great-Great Grandfather losing his dance tunic. Wondering about that, Daniel finally fell into a deep sleep.

2
Crab

"Come 'ere, Danny, I've got something to show you." Daniel was doing the breakfast dishes while Leonard went to work in his studio.

In the middle of the studio, taking up most of the length of the room, was a long, sleek cedar canoe, maybe eighteen feet long, balanced on wooden braces. Daniel walked slowly next to it, running his hand along the smooth, oiled sides.

Leonard explained how it came about. "You remember the commission I left Hannah Island for after Mother died? The dugout canoe? Well, after we finished that, there was a big chunk of cedar left over. I used it to make this two-man canoe."

Daniel thought back to the day when Leonard left for

Seattle. He remembered it as rainy and gloomy. Leonard, however, seemed unaware of that darkness. He appeared animated and happy describing how five young apprentices had carved the fifty-foot dugout canoe, like the one in the wedding story, under the direction of their "master," Charlie Amber. Charlie was an elder like Grandfather who knew the stories of his people first-hand.

As it was the night before, Daniel was glad to listen. It gave him some relief from his worries. When would Leonard be taking him back to Grandfather? *Today?* Even if he could avoid telling Leonard, he knew he eventually would have to tell Grandfather: how he had lived on the streets for weeks without getting in touch with Leonard, how he had hoped to impress his brother with the money he had earned, how it had turned out. *Lousy*, he thought.

Leonard went on painting the canoe scene. "Charlie would call up his spirit helper whenever we needed guidance. He said an owl—that's what his spirit helper is—would lead us to the cedar. And it did—one that must have drifted away from a log boom—beached not very far up the coast. Then Charlie asked his helper, which tool would we use to remove the bark? How would we shape the outside and then hollow the inside of the massive trunk?"

After weeks of burning and chiseling, Leonard continued, Charlie called on his spirit helper again to find rocks for steaming the canoe into shape. When they had found the right ones, they had built a fire and heated the rocks until they glowed red. That way the water inside the canoe heated up. After shaping the canoe, they had sanded it smooth and rubbed it with fish oil.

For a moment, Daniel's mind flashed back to the streets. It was just yesterday that he had used shoe polish to put a quick finish on the carving for the tourist lady.

"I planned on using the smaller canoe to explore the Inside Passage sometime, maybe go try to find Great-Great Grandmother's island."

Daniel was taken aback. Didn't Leonard remember the plans *they* had made back home before Leonard got the commission in Seattle? Daniel recalled it well. How they had rowed around the harbor in a little metal rowboat talking about their plans—getting themselves some camping gear, maybe even carving their own dugout canoe, exploring the beaches and rainforests on the islands of the Inside Passage, looking for the ruins of longhouses, totem poles and burial boxes.

"Danny, let's do it now. You and me."

Despite his disappointment, Daniel was conscious of a tiny bubble of enthusiasm rising in his stomach.

"So, Danny, will you go with me?"

"O.K. Yeah, I'd go."

* * *

The next day, sitting in the passenger seat of his brother's car, Daniel had little to say. He stared out the window, watching a blur of gray go by—building after building—then a blur of green—tree after tree. This is the way things started to look when Mother died, he thought. He remembered how Leonard and Grandfather had cried and carried on, but for him it was different. Daniel had just stopped seeing things clearly, as if he were looking through one of the shards of smoky green glass he collected on the beach. And when Leonard left for Seattle, a few months later, it was as if the glass had been crushed.

As they drove, his thoughts were slivers festering in his mind: *Just when things start looking up—selling those carvings—I end up in jail! If I tell Leonard I didn't steal the money, what if he doesn't believe me?*

Two ferries and a long car ride later, cedar canoe strapped to the roof of the car, they entered a fishing town, Stewart's Landing. This would be the putting-in point for their voyage up the passage. Daniel started getting nervous. Nothing had gone right since he left Grandfather. Why would it be any different now? Would he be able to pull his weight? Would he be embarrassed again in front of his brother?

He didn't get any more time to fret. They parked the car and headed to the general store to buy a few last minute supplies, then back to the car for the canoe. The canoe was heavy, and in what Daniel saw to be his first test of strength, he resisted the urge to put his end of the canoe down before reaching the water.

At the beach, they found a spot without any large rocks. "Watch how you put your end down!" Leonard's voice was tense. Then they saw how buoyant and stable the canoe was in the water, and Leonard added with relief, "Let's take this baby for a spin."

The sun was getting low on the horizon. Leonard pointed out to sea and said, "According to my map, Danny, there's a good place to camp on the island you can see beyond the inlet."

"Now, get in but stay low," Leonard continued. "Once you get the hang of paddling, you'll sit in the bow because you're lighter. But for now I've shifted the gear to the stern so that I can sit in front and you can watch me."

Daniel climbed into the boat and crouched down in the stern. Then Leonard pushed the canoe away from the shore as he jumped in and made his way hand over hand to the bow. When Leonard dipped his paddle into the quiet water and pulled, Daniel felt the canoe gently lift and glide. For a few moments Daniel watched his brother paddle. The silhouette that Leonard made against the sunlight, with his straight hair loose and flowing over his broad muscled shoulders, made him think of the ancestors in Grandfather's stories. Then, as Daniel got caught up in the rhythm created by Leonard's paddle slicing the glassy water, he started to paddle himself. After awhile, paddling in exact unison with his brother, and making as little splash as possible, were the only things that mattered.

In little more than an hour, they approached a small island where they would spend the night. It was one of twin islands, separated by a narrow band of water, each with a pure white beach, composed of millions of tiny shards of shells.

Leonard instructed Daniel on how to turn the canoe around. They would beach the canoe stern first in order to protect the cut-water bow. Paddling in reverse, they let the stern of the canoe slide up onto the beach.

Now with the sun setting behind the tall firs, as soon as they carried the canoe to a safe place above the high water mark, they set out to locate a campsite. In no time, they found a spot on a grassy knoll overlooking the small channel between the islands. Too tired to build a campfire or start the cook stove, they shared some bread, cheese and fruit they had purchased at the general store, and then they settled into their sleeping bags inside their "one-man tents". With the zippered openings facing the channel, Daniel gazed at the huge old madrona tree reaching way out over the water. *It'll stand watch while we sleep,* he mused. Too tired to do any thinking—or fretting—he drifted off to sleep.

When he opened his eyes the next morning, the deep pink morning light bathed everything around them—the eagle sitting on the madrona scanning the water below, the seal perched on a rock nibbling on a crab. When the brothers began to stir, the seal slipped into the water, leaving the half-eaten crab, which the eagle immediately swooped down to take advantage of. And then Daniel realized that what were two islands in the high tide of the night were actually one in the low tide of the morning.

"Hey, Leonard, I bet I can get us a crab for breakfast just by dipping my hand into that tide pool."

"OK, I'll boil some water," Leonard said, as Daniel headed down toward the beach.

Daniel kneeled down on a large rock at the edge of the pool and examined the occupants, two purple starfish and one big, bright orange crab. He positioned his hand over the water just above where the crab sat and then plunged it into the pool. He was amazed at what he brought up—not a tasty crab but an inedible starfish. The crab was nowhere in sight. Daniel made his way back up the slope and for a split second he remembered what he had felt like in Seattle. But at the top of the slope he was greeted by the aroma of the oatmeal Leonard was cooking on the camp stove.

"So, you didn't think I could do it, did you?" he said to Leonard, as he approached holding up his empty hands. "Well, I'm glad cuz I'm starved!"

They set out after breakfast and got into the rhythm of paddling, moving smoothly through the placid water of late summer. They paddled until their arms were tired or until they got hungry. Then they would stop at the closest little island to have a snack or to rest on the beach.

The only interruptions came from what stirred around them. Seals popping their heads out of the water, watching them with big, soft eyes. A peregrine falcon leaving its nest on a cliff side to make lightening-fast dives for the little black and white seabirds with orange feet—Daniel had never seen them before—that seemed to be the favorite food of its squawking young.

That afternoon they were in a race with four Dall's porpoises.

"Let's go for it, Leonard!" Daniel shouted, as the porpoises came up from behind.

The brothers started paddling as fast as they could as the small Dall's porpoises, two on each side, jetted past them and sprayed them as they arched through the air ahead of the canoe. The black and white marks on the porpoises' bodies became a whorl of grays when they shot into the air and twisted just before they splashed back into the water. Then the porpoises disappeared.

While Leonard was drying off his face with his sleeve and Daniel was exclaiming, "Wow, was that a short race!" the porpoises reappeared behind them. They had returned to the "starting line" by swimming underwater beneath the canoe. Over and over again the porpoises did this, and each time Daniel and Leonard tried racing with them.

Finally, Leonard shouted laughingly to the tireless porpoises, "You win! You'd keep this up all day!"

"Oh, come on, Leonard! One more time!" Daniel cried, as he dug his paddle in with all the strength he had left. Leonard responded, and they went at it once more.

When the porpoises passed the canoe this time, they made their biggest splash yet. But rather than returning to the "starting line" as they had before, the porpoises kept going. Daniel and Leonard, buckled over from exhaustion, looked up and smiled to see the winners dancing with abandon into the horizon.

At dinnertime, Leonard said, "So, Danny, tonight we

have a choice of cracked crab or reconstituted dried mashed potatoes. Which is your pleasure?"

"Oh, right, Leonard, I'm really gonna pass up crab!" Daniel's mouth watered over the idea of feasting on the sweet boiled crab that he had been hankering for. But first they had to catch it.

They paddled out to deep water to set out a crab pot filled with the dried chum they had bought at the general store on the mainland. An hour later when they paddled back out to pull up the pot, Leonard smiled and said, "Hopefully, this will work better than your hand-dipping method, Danny."

Pointing at the water's surface, he said, "Go ahead and grab the buoy and then pull up on the rope."

Hand over fist, Daniel gradually hauled in the crab pot. When it appeared on the surface, it was jam packed with crabs, legs and claws thrashing all over, each crab trying to escape over the top of the other.

"Good," Leonard said. "There are way too many crabs for dinner, so Danny, now you can set most of them free. Keep the largest."

Daniel managed to unclamp some claws and open the cage door. Glancing at Leonard to make sure he was using the right technique, he began to put his hand into the tangle to pick out the smallest to set free.

"Grab them from behind, or you'll lose a finger!" Leonard exclaimed.

As Daniel pulled one of the smaller crabs out of the cage, he watched it sink into the sea with its legs spread wide, as if in slow motion, enjoying its freedom. When only four large crabs were left in the crab pot, the brothers paddled back to shore.

Leonard started the camp stove and put a pot of water on to boil.

"Are you going to drop the crabs into the boiling water alive?" Daniel asked, having watched his mother do this before.

Leonard replied, "That's one way to do it, but not the best. For the best flavor, you kill the crab first and clean it before dropping it into boiling water. Here's how." Leonard took a struggling crab out of the cage and turned it over, showing Daniel the spot where he would aim the club.

Daniel wondered where had Leonard learned this method. In college? In Europe? He'd have to ask him later.

"Danny, you hit it hard and fast and it will die without pain. Go ahead," Leonard said.

Placing the crab on its back on the ground, Daniel picked up the thick branch he would use as a club and aimed it at the helpless crab. He stood there for a few seconds and then lowered the club in exasperation.

"I can't do it, Leonard," Daniel exclaimed. "What if I don't do it right and the crab doesn't die right away?"

"OK, let me do the first one," Leonard said. "I remember how tricky it was the first time I tried it." Picking up the club, he killed it with a decisive whack. Then he handed the club back to Daniel.

This time Daniel was able to execute the task perfectly, and went on to complete the job. After cleaning the crabs by removing the innards in the saltwater at the beach, Daniel dropped them into the boiling water. In a few minutes, they were ready to eat.

When Daniel cracked open a crab leg and sucked a morsel of meat out of it, the taste was even sweeter than he had anticipated.

* * *

That night, in a sleeping bag under the stars, Daniel had the sensation that he was still floating on the water. His body felt as though it were being gently rocked. But his mind was tossing him to and fro between home, Seattle and this remote island. So many changes since the eagle stared him in the eye. What will be next? *Maybe I should I tell Leonard what really happened?*

Then, falling asleep, he imagined what it would be like to be in space, floating in a canoe from star to star.

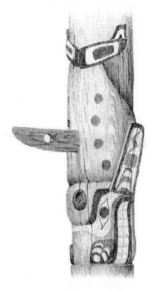

3
Whale

The morning of the third day was different. A fog shrouded the harbor and made their skin damp and chilled as they crawled out of their tents. After they cleaned up camp and stowed their gear in the canoe, Leonard stood on the beach looking out into the grayness.

"Danny, looks like we'll have to wait until the fog lifts." Just as Daniel came up from behind, they heard a sound like steam spouting from a geyser, coming from somewhere out in the water. They looked at each other and, without a moment's hesitation, jumped into the canoe and started paddling through the fog toward that sound.

When the fog opened slightly, what emerged from the grayness, only a few feet away from the canoe, was a huge black and white Orca whale with its head tilted upward, halfway out of the water, eyeing them. The canoe was so close to the whale that Daniel got a whiff of the whale's fishy breath. And he could peer into his mouth, a mouth that appeared as wide as the prow of the canoe. The cone-shaped teeth, each as tall as Daniel's thumb, encircled the whale's jaw like a giant necklace.

Through a break in the fog, Daniel caught a glimpse of other whales and he realized they had encountered a whole pod of Orcas.

They'll lead us through the fog, Daniel thought, as he looked into the whale's knowing eye. Then the Orca dove ahead, disappearing momentarily. Steering in the stern, Daniel tried to maneuver the canoe around to follow. But the whale's dive had caused the sea to swell, and water rushed over the bow. Struggling to stabilize the canoe, they paddled hard directly into the waves. The brothers' pulling action, deep into the water and perfectly "in synch," transported the canoe cleanly through the wave. Yet, now they found themselves in the center of a whirlpool created by the whale's disappearing bulk. The canoe was seriously tilting—and Daniel's heart was racing. He was in unfamiliar waters, but he glad he was in the stern so he could mimic Leonard's technique. When their paddles were extended rigidly on either side of the canoe, he felt the canoe rolling back to center. He heaved a sigh of relief.

Now joining the procession, the brothers paddled as fast as they could. Then when they realized they were being swept along in the Orca's slipstream, they relaxed into an easy pace. That gave Daniel a chance to count the whales—twelve in all including a baby—swimming behind their leader alongside the canoe. Their huge bodies undulated up and down; their long fins cut through the water like swords. Daniel began to feel as if the canoe were just another member of the pod. It wasn't long before they were able to recognize individuals. There were momma and baby, of course, and an aunt or an uncle that stayed between the baby and the canoe. Momma's body would bob out of the water and then a moment later baby would pop up just behind her.

"Hey, Leonard, you can tell the whales apart by the their fins, the different shapes and marks," Daniel said, now feeling comfortable with these imposing escorts.

Leonard agreed. "Look at the fin on the big guy. It looks like he's been in a fight or two." Daniel could imagine the skirmishes that left the almost man-sized dorsal fin so deeply notched.

"Wolves of the sea," Leonard explained, the Orcas had no real rivals, not even sharks. Except that, on occasion, the pod would encounter a maverick, a lone Orca, attempting to maraud their territory. A fight might ensue.

Maybe they deserve their reputation, Daniel thought, *but I feel safe with them swimming alongside us.*

Leonard voiced that same feeling. "As long as they stay with us in the fog, I'm not worried about the canoe colliding with a ship or drifting into a dangerous current."

The brothers and the whales were together most of the morning. Then, when the fog began to lift, the whales started swimming faster. Gradually they left the canoe behind. The whales' loud "blows" turned into faint sighs and their bodies shrank into black dots on the horizon.

Although Leonard had been carefully mapping out their journey, Daniel was aware that this interlude with the whales took them on an uncharted course. Yet somehow it felt as if the whales had dropped them off just where they should be. In the distance they spotted an island, one that had a different aspect from the others they had visited. It looked dull and barren. Nevertheless, they could see the vague outline of buildings along the rim of the shore with tall poles lined up in front like sentries.

"Danny, the island up ahead might be Great-Great Grandmother's island, the one in the story—where the wedding took place."

Leonard stopped paddling and stared ahead for a long time. Then, without another word to Daniel, he took a plank out from the floor of the canoe and placed it on top of the gunwales. He jumped up on the plank and, balancing deftly, started waving his arms up and down, slowly flexing and releasing his muscles.

"Hey, Eagle," Daniel said to Leonard, "looks like your wings aren't working too good today!"

When Leonard didn't seem to hear him, Daniel realized that something he didn't quite understand was going on.

Leonard started making a low throaty chanting sound, "Ha, hey, he, yah, ha. Ha, hey, yah."

As his brother's arms pulsated in a steady rhythm, Daniel watched, spellbound. Leonard became more and more caught up in his movement. Then, like Great-Great Grandfather in the story of his wedding, Leonard started to do the Eagle dance. Daniel paddled to the tempo of the dancing and chanting, and then he found himself joining in with soft chanting sounds himself. He kept paddling and Leonard kept dancing until they approached the shore.

What they experienced as their canoe slid up onto the sandy beach was nothing like what happened in the wedding story.

Instead of being greeted by happy people singing and drumming, Daniel and Leonard were welcomed only by the wind whistling through beams and poles, the ghostly remains of a settlement.

Lined up along a rocky promontory were four carved mortuary posts. Vegetation was now growing out of the decayed ends of the posts and only a vague outline of the carved figures—animal, man or monster, Daniel couldn't tell—remained. The burial boxes they had once contained were long gone, swept away in a storm or gradually eaten away by the elements.

As they walked slowly toward the moss-covered ruins of buildings, Daniel asked, "So you think this where Great-Great Grandmother came from, Leonard?"

"It could be; what's left looks like the kind of village in Grandfather's stories. But I don't know exactly where the island was. And even if I did, I admit I don't know exactly where we are, where the whales took us."

"Leonard, why did everyone leave here?" Daniel hoped the answer would take away the emptiness he felt.

"Smallpox. You know, Danny, I don't know for sure. But it was probably smallpox disease that came with the European settlers."

"Like the TB that Mother had? Did everyone die? Even the white people?" Daniel asked.

"It's even more contagious than TB. No, mostly the Indians died. They didn't have immunity to those killer germs," Leonard replied, shaking his head.

Daniel picked up a rock and threw it with a vengeance at one of the cedar posts. Then he let loose a stream of obscenities, accompanied by a list of everything he felt he hated. The cops in Seattle. The white settlers. The smallpox that killed his ancestors. The TB that killed his mother.

Unable to stop, he picked up rock after rock and flung them at whatever he saw. Finally, he reeled around and aimed a rock at the canoe. With a hollow "thunk" the rock bounced off the canoe's side. Daniel saw that it left a small gash in the canoe's smooth wood.

A faint echo returned along with a raven's resounding "Quok!"

Tears came running down Daniel's face.

He blurted out, "I didn't steal that money!"

Leonard replied softly, "I believe you, Danny."

"I sold some carvings and I was feeling good. So I started running and they thought I was running away! Those buttheads!"

Leonard said haltingly, "Danny—the day I left you after Mother died—I didn't want to go. I wanted to stay with you and Grandfather. After Mother died, I wanted to spend time with you, teach you some carving, help Grandfather take care of stuff. But I didn't tell you how bad I felt about leaving. I guess I thought I might not be able to leave if I did."

He paused and his eyes closed for a moment, as if picturing that day. "Maybe I should have stayed." Then, straightening up slightly, he continued, "But you know, the opportunity I had—the dugout canoe—even Grandfather thought I shouldn't pass that up. He worried about how hurt you'd be. I guess that's why he let you go to Seattle. Danny, I'm sorry I didn't talk to you before I left. I'm sorry I left."

Putting his hand on his brother's arm, he said again, "I *am* sorry, Danny."

Daniel pulled his arm away from his brother and, sobbing now, covered his face with his hands. Through his sobs, he said, "They even took away the carving knife Grandfather gave me. They said it might be a weapon!"

Leonard reached into his jeans pocket and took out a small leather case. He put it into his brother's tear-stained hand. "Danny, take this one. It was Father's. He'd want you to have it."

Daniel felt the curve of the small knife through the well-worn deerskin. Looking directly at his brother, he stammered as his sobs subsided, "I ...I just wanted to show you I could make money on my carvings."

He had said it. And Leonard had believed him. Yet, now Daniel felt like nothing was left inside of him.

The brothers stood in the wind, their own feelings mirrored by the gray weather and the loneliness of the abandoned village around them.

After a few minutes, Leonard broke the silence. "Come on. Let's take a look at these ruins and try to imagine what Great-Great Grandmother's house might have looked like."

They walked up the beach and came upon what could have been the ruins of the longhouse where Great-Great Grandmother's family had held the wedding celebration. There were a couple of huge moss-covered cross beams, with the rows of chiseling still evident, leaning against corner posts. It looked like the outline of an extremely large building, with an excavated square in the center. The brothers walked the perimeter—yes, this might have been the very place where Great-Great Grandfather danced on his wedding night.

"Imagine, Danny," Leonard said, as he walked between the posts into the longhouse, holding his arms wide at his sides, "that we're walking through a doorway made of a great carved totem pole."

Daniel observed that Leonard bent forward a bit as if not wanting to hit his head on the imaginary doorframe.

Leonard continued. "The opening is shaped like a person's

mouth, big enough to walk through if you stoop down. At the top of the pole a raven signifies Great-Great Grandmother's clan. Her family would have been proud to invite Great-Great Grandfather and his family into their home through this doorway the night of the wedding."

The brothers walked over to a grassy ledge and sat down. They were sitting on what would have been the platform overlooking the fire pit and center stage.

They watched blades of beach grass dance in the wind.

* * *

Under the gray sky, with a chill of fog still in the air, they headed up the beach away from the ruins.

"Don't you think it's too quiet here?" Leonard asked. "It could be the fog, but something else is strange." He turned away from the water and stepped from rock to rock up toward the driftwood on the perimeter of the beach. Daniel followed behind.

It was here that Leonard came upon the bones. A pile of large bones. Bones too big and thick to be human, he said. Too massive and not long enough to be deer. They crouched down to examine them.

Picking up one of the largest, Leonard said, "They look like the bones of a large bear, Danny."

Then he scanned down the rest of the beach and cried, "My God, there are piles of bones all along this beach! It's as if all the animals on the island ended up dying here."

Daniel's mind began searching for an explanation and he asked, "Leonard, do animals get smallpox?"

"No, it's only a human disease. And from the looks of these bones, whatever happened, happened not very long ago."

Chills ran up and down Daniel's spine.

His brother continued. "Let's hike up into the forest and see if we can figure out what's going on."

The beach was at the bottom of an 80-foot rock face so they had to explore for a way to get to the top.

"I may need to go back to the canoe to get my rock-climbing gear." Leonard said.

But Daniel had found some rocks that were graduated and acted as steps. He was already scrambling up the cliff by gripping rocky protrusions and branches that were growing between the cracks. He was well on his way to the top when Leonard began his deliberate ascent.

There at the top, a scene of utter desolation assaulted Daniel. As far as his eyes could see, it was gray. A desert of stumps—some as tall as a man and up to ten feet in diameter, others just under a foot across. His mind swirled in confusion. How could his ancestors' beautiful rainforest have turned into something that looked more like the surface of the moon?

When Leonard reached the top, he gasped. After a few moments, he said, "What we're looking at is a complete clear-cut of the entire island."

Miles of barren moonscape lay before them. Although appearing lifeless, there were actually tiny alder trees struggling to grow between the ruins of what had been magnificent cedars and spruce and fir. Neither Leonard nor Daniel could utter a word. As they stumbled over blackberry vines and beer cans, Daniel felt as if his breath had been sucked from his body.

When Leonard finally spoke, he sounded as if were reading from a textbook. "The clear-cut destroyed the shelter of the animals as well as their food source. If we take a look at the streams running through this island, we won't find any salmon. The water—"

"Did salmon stop coming back just because there were no trees?"

"Well, they came back to spawn, but the water would have gotten too silty and warm when all the trees were cut along the banks. Some of the salmon wouldn't have made it up stream. And, then, the eggs of those that did make it were destroyed by the heat and mud."

"Did the bears die because there were no more salmon to eat?"

"Not right away," Leonard said. "The strongest ones swam away from the island, across the passage to the mainland. But when the salmon stopped coming, the old bears, and the very young ones, gradually lost too much weight to survive the winters. Especially since they started the winter underweight, with fewer berries to eat during the summer. The eagles and other birds went elsewhere but the bears and other mammals on the island were stranded. From the piles of bones we saw on the beach, we can figure they died searching the seashore for food."

"When?" Daniel asked.

"Judging from the size of the alders, this must have happened 3 or 4 years ago. Wolves probably survived longer, but the wolves must have finished off the last deer and rodents and rabbits and then they too died. Of course, the loggers probably did their share of hunting before they left."

* * *

That night, in his tent next to his brother's near the ruins, Daniel's mind was filled with ghastly images of scrawny bears prowling the beach. He understood how desperate the bears felt, turning over every rock, discovering nothing. Then he thought back to telling Leonard what had happened in Seattle.

Leonard had believed him, but Daniel couldn't understand why he now felt empty instead of relieved. Wondering whether the bears had fought each other over the last crab, he fell into a fitful sleep.

4
Seal

They didn't look back. The next morning, as the brothers shoved the canoe away from the shore and the sun began to warm the day, Daniel's mood brightened. It was as if his anger had lifted with the fog.

Every stroke of the paddle was taking him farther away from Seattle. Funny how desperately he had wanted to stay in Seattle with Leonard. Now all he knew was that he wanted to keep going. He wanted to discover what adventure would be next. Would it be another escort by whales? Another race with porpoises? Or maybe an encounter with some animals on the next island?

Bears?

Just as he was twisting around to tell Leonard what he

wanted, he became aware that Leonard had stopped paddling and was pouring over his map. Daniel drew a shallow breath and held it. Was Leonard charting a way back to Stewart's Landing now that they had found Great-Great Grandmother's island?

"I have a pretty good idea of where we are. I just need to see if the next islands up north look like I expect them to look," Leonard said.

Daniel exhaled in relief. They weren't going back.

Leonard explained that as long as they continued going north and kept some islands to the west of them, they would remain in the more protected waters. The real danger would be leaving the 'inside passage' and finding themselves in open ocean.

Passing by the two islands to the north, Daniel again noticed that Leonard had stopped paddling. Daniel set his own paddle on the gunwale and turned to face Leonard.

Leonard was scanning the horizon. His eyes came to rest on something off in the distance. "Danny, the next island is going to be incredible." Then Leonard's brow furrowed for a moment. "Unless, that is, a logging company has gotten there first. "

"Do you remember Grandfather's story about the Island of the Ghost Bear?" Leonard asked.

"Sure," Daniel was quick to respond. "But you mean it really exists? I thought it was just a story, you know, like how Raven turned the black bear white and the gray wolves black."

"Well, that's part of the legend. But there really exists an island like that. And last I read it was still untouched by civilization. We could be there by lunch time."

Island of the Ghost Bear. Daniel repeated the name over

and over in his mind. The Ghost Bear story was the best his Grandfather told. Many times, walking along the beach on Hannah Island, he had imagined what the white bear looked like. He thought back to the carvings he had done—carvings of Raven turning the bear white. Especially the one he sold to the tourist lady in Seattle. He wondered if she had hung it on her living room wall as she said she would.

But he never, ever, imagined that the Ghost Bear actually existed.

Then, he became aware of Leonard gripping his paddle and digging it in hard, as if now in a big hurry.

After an hour of vigorous paddling, they could make out an expansive island surrounded by a glowing mist, as if it had its own atmosphere. Then, closer, it appeared so radiantly green in the noonday sun that the water around it shimmered like turquoise.

Entering a sheltered cove, they were greeted by a flurry of activity. Seabirds were everywhere, some floating serenely on the water and then disappearing with a tiny splash in a blink of the eye, others slowly taking off with a pattering of wings on the water, and still others diving from an approach high in the air. Blue-black cormorants were standing on rocky outcroppings, hanging their wings out to their sides to dry like feathery laundry.

Close to shore, a four-foot tall Great Blue Heron was standing immobile on one leg in the shallow water, looking almost prehistoric. When the canoe drew near, he gave the brothers a weary look and took off on gangly oversized wings. His loud croak of complaint as he unsteadily took flight made Daniel think, *This could be the first bird that ever flew.*

"Danny, let's set up camp here. We'll want to stay for awhile and explore," Leonard announced as they slid the canoe backwards up on to the pebbly beach.

Daniel jumped out of the canoe into the shallow water and was surprised to feel that the water was warm enough to swim in. The protected cove had been warmed by the late summer sun and had risen to an unusually high temperature for these northern waters. He pulled off his tee shirt and with a shallow dive plunged into the crystal clear water.

Coming up with a splash, he challenged, "Leonard, come on in! You don't need to start working yet! If you don't get in the water, I'm gonna drag you in!"

Leonard kept unloading the canoe, but then he too took off his tee shirt and dove into the water. Swimming under water for a time, he came to the surface with a look of relief.

"Danny, this island is still untouched! Just you wait and see what amazing things it has in store for us."

Maybe still untouched, but would they find a Ghost Bear?

They lost track of time dog-paddling around and floating on their backs to soak up the sunshine. When they found themselves floating in the midst of a giant kelp grove, they propelled themselves through the water by grabbing hold of the hollow bulbs bobbing on the surface. The kelp was like a marine forest, and the brothers were swimming in the canopy. Daniel dove down to try to follow the kelp "trunk" to the bottom but came back up breathless some moments later.

He was surprised to see a little seal watching him from only a few feet away. All Daniel could see of the seal was his whiskered round head and bright eyes. When Daniel paddled in one direction, the seal moved effortlessly in that same direction, always keeping his eyes fixed on Daniel's. Daniel swam in the other direction—the seal moved with him. Even when Daniel raised his head out of the water, the seal did the same. Daniel and the seal moved as if they were mirror images of each other.

Leonard started laughing. "Hey, little brother, the seal's more graceful," he said. "But you're cuter."

"Thanks, Leonard!" Daniel sucked in a deep breath and dove again, the seal still following him. He opened his eyes under water and glimpsed the seal disappearing into deep water. Without surfacing, Daniel swam up next to Leonard and yanked on Leonard's leg, pulling him under. Leonard rotated under water and reached to grab Daniel's arm but Daniel slipped away. Daniel came up gulping for air, and immediately started searching for Leonard, above and below the surface of the water, knowing he was in for a counter attack. There was no sign of him. Suddenly, he felt Leonard's grip on both his ankles. Keeping his body rigid, Daniel felt himself being shot out of the water. He came down on his back with a big splash like an Orca breaching. He recovered quickly, held his breath and swam under water back towards Leonard for his own turn at retaliation. But when Daniel surfaced, he saw that Leonard's powerful crawl-stroke had taken him well out of reach.

Recovering from their antics, Daniel swam slowly toward the beach and spied a mother deer and her fawns eyeing them curiously from the forest. From the leisurely manner they were making their way up the steep cliff side, Daniel surmised that the deer on this island had never been hunted.

And all along, the seabirds continued to go about business as usual.

Finally, when hunger made the brothers head for the beach, they dallied a while longer by stretching out on a couple of large flat rocks that had been warmed by the sun.

"Leonard, this place is the best. Let's stay here a long time," Daniel murmured. "We could eat fish and crab and berries and some greens from the forest, couldn't we?"

"Well, Danny, I'm sure we could figure out how to survive

here, especially with the fall salmon beginning to spawn soon. But, hey, don't forget that the rainy season's almost here. Once it starts, you'll feel different. Anyway, we brought enough food to last for a couple more weeks, but we need to conserve enough to get back to Stewart's Landing...."

"But, Leonard, let's stay as long as we can, OK?"

"Sure, we can do that."

* * *

That night, when it was time to settle down to sleep, Daniel didn't feel like getting into his tent. His first taste of this island made him too energized to sleep. Instead, he spread his sleeping bag out in front of his tent and lay on his back gazing up at the stars. In the moonless sky, the stars were dazzling. Focusing, Daniel picked out a shooting star. Then another. After a minute, he had counted twenty. Then twenty more. After a half hour or so, he had counted two hundred and he thought, *This can't be real! Where did all these shooting stars come from? Leonard will know.* So he woke his brother up. "Leonard, what is a shooting star, anyway? And why are there so many tonight?"

Leonard had just fallen asleep. When he opened his eyes, he looked surprised by the brightness of the sky. Yawning, he answered, "That's the Perseids, Danny." He joined Daniel in stargazing.

Daniel repeated, "Perseids." "Two hundred and one. Two hundred and two. Two hundred and three..."

Leonard explained, "Around the middle of August, the earth orbits through a part of space that's filled with space dust, maybe like the pebbles on the beach. And because we're far from any lights and we're in the north—we can see this so well. It's a meteor shower. It—"

"Two hundred and ten. Grandfather says shooting stars come from Raven's torch when he leads dead people away. Two hundred and eleven. The shooting stars are like, uh…"

"Embers," Leonard offered.

"Two hundred and twelve. Yeah, like embers falling from the torch as he leads the dead people. Do meteors ever hit the earth, Leonard?"

"Not often, Danny, but there have been some large meteors that have done that, and they left huge craters miles wide."

* * *

Falling asleep, Daniel was still counting shooting stars, not sure whether he was awake or dreaming. Already he sensed that on the Island of the Ghost Bear it would be hard to tell.

5
Bear

Ghost Bears. Leonard had said they'd be on the island. He said he read they were still there, but mostly he just knew it. So when they started exploring the next day, Daniel expected Leonard to look for signs.

But Daniel became distracted by the other amusements that this island offered. Right in front of his eyes. Never had he seen trees like this. The island where he and his brother grew up had been logged repeatedly, so, at best, the trees were a couple of feet wide when they were cut again. It made them easy to climb, which these monsters wouldn't be. Yes, these trees, especially the cedars, looked to Daniel like the hairy legs of silent monsters. Their enormous claws gripped the mossy earth as they walked. Daniel thought he could never climb

these trees as he climbed at home, without equipment, even ropes; he could hardly see the first set of limbs. And the canopy was so high and thick that only a bird could enjoy the sunlight. For those below, in this primeval forest, sunlight was a rare thing.

So Daniel wasn't paying much attention to Leonard examining the tracks in the soil.

"They're large," Leonard was saying, "but the claws are close to the toes and slightly curved. They're the tracks of a black bear not a Grizzly."

Daniel heard the words but didn't register their meaning. Maybe he'd get an idea of how to climb one of these monsters by starting with a spruce nearby.

"Look at these trees," Leonard was saying as he examined the spruce and hemlock seedlings. "They look like victims of a battering, what's left of them."

On larger trees, bark had been scraped off in a vertical pattern extending high up the tree. "Only a large animal with claws, one that likes to climb, could make those marks so high up on the trunks. Yep, that's a black bear, not a Grizzly."

"Hey, Danny, look at this black scat full of berry seeds. It's still steaming," Leonard said. "Danny! Where did you go? I'm pretty sure there's a—"

"Watch this, Leonard!" Leonard looked up to see Daniel swinging out on a spruce limb aiming to land on the top of a huge, decaying cedar stump. Daniel didn't realize it would be hollow inside.

Just before reaching his target, the bough Daniel was swinging on snapped off and he fell from a height of about fifteen feet onto the spongy ground. A little dazed, he lay still on his back. When he lifted his head and looked up, he was gazing into the black eyes of a large white bear peering over the edge of the hollow stump.

From a branch nearby, a raven made a series of clicking sounds, like the ticking of an alarm clock, as if counting out the seconds that were passing.

The white bear looked at him calmly, hopped out of the hollowed stump and scurried up a tree nearby. He sat in a branch looking down at Daniel. After a few moments, he dangled his front leg down towards Daniel, as if reaching out to him. There was nothing but curiosity in his eyes. And Daniel knew it.

Leonard watched the scene for almost a minute, not making any sudden noise, and then edged closer. When he reached Daniel, he pulled him to his feet and they began slowly backing off until the bear was out of sight.

When they reached their campsite, Daniel was bursting with excitement.

"That was the Ghost Bear, wasn't it, Leonard? He wasn't afraid of us? Did you see how he looked at me? Were you afraid of him? I don't think I was!" Daniel chattered.

Leonard kept shaking his head in disbelief. He spoke fast, at first almost in a whisper, with half an ear focused on the sounds in the forest.

"I can't believe what we saw. How could we have found the Ghost Bear, and what a situation! At first I thought you were in trouble—sprawled on the ground looking up at a big bear. What were you doing swinging from branches, anyway? Do you think you're a chimpanzee? Wrong forest, little brother. No wonder the bear was amazed."

Both brothers laughed, now beginning to relive their astonishing experience with the friendly white bear.

Daniel asked, "How did white bear get to this island? I know what the story said, but did they actually swim from Alaska?"

"No, these bears have always been here. They aren't polar bears, they're black bears, like the ones at home. Once in a while a black bear is born white. But very, very seldom. Except here on this island."

Daniel asked, "Why this island?"

"It's because the bear population has been limited and over thousands of years the recessive white gene has become more prevalent. Scientists say that about one bear in every ten is white, here. They call them Kermode bears after the guy who 'discovered' them. But you and I know that Indians have always known about these white bears, 'moskgm'ol,' they called them."

"So, what do you mean by recess...something genes? Like the jeans you wear for recess?" Daniel asked.

Leonard continued. "Genes are the instructions that your body uses to grow into whatever you're going to be. They determine whether you are tall or short, a girl or a boy, whether your hair is brown or black. Same thing with a bear."

"What about the recess part?" Daniel asked, serious now.

"Recessive. Genes either have a lot of influence on what you're like—the dominant ones—or less influence—the recessive ones. In order for the recessive ones to show up, they need to be— "

"I don't get it, Leonard," Daniel said.

"Well, let's see, there's something else. You and I have similar genes because we have the same mother and father. Our mother gave us one gene, our father another for each trait we have. It takes two genes to make up one trait like color."

Leonard explained that white is a recessive trait, and for a recessive trait like white to show up in a bear, both the mother and the father bear had to contribute a white gene.

"Now it's more likely that a white bear will mate with

another white bear, or with another bear with a white gene, on a relatively small island than it is on the mainland. It's a small gene pool."

"OK, I sort of get it," Daniel said. But then, feeling mischievous, he added, "So you wear small jeans when you're in a pool."

"Forget it, Danny. Go back to swinging in trees for all you understand!" Leonard laughingly replied.

"I'm starving, Leonard! Let's catch some salmon for dinner. Didn't you say they'd be spawning soon? Maybe they're back."

"Let's go check out a stream. I think it's early—it hasn't rained enough but it's worth a look," Leonard said as he scanned up and down the beach for the mouth of a stream.

"Remember, Danny, we'll have to share the salmon with the bears and eagles and osprey and maybe even wolves."

Walking down the beach towards the stream, the brothers continued their conversation.

"Leonard, don't you think that white bear was actually friendly? He didn't seem afraid at all."

Leonard nodded his head in agreement. "Or she? The bear looked young, so that might explain some of it. But also, as far as we know, nobody lives on this island. Or ever has. And so it's likely that no one has ever hunted these bears. Maybe what they call an instinctive fear of man isn't true. But we don't know if this bear is an exception. Anyway, we still need to be careful, because even here, a mother bear with cubs will be protective."

When they got to the stream, the huge rocks were dry, with only trickles of water flowing through the streambed. No salmon. And that was as it should be. Even the mighty salmon wouldn't have been able to navigate the dry rocks had they arrived before the rains.

As they filled their water bottles with fresh water, Leonard said, "We'll have mussels instead. It's low tide and they covered the rocks along the beach."

Then he added with a smile, "We'll survive."

"OK, but I wanna catch a salmon as soon as they get here."

* * *

As the brothers sat around the camp stove on the beach cracking open mussel shells, they gazed at the familiar sea. Behind them, cormorants were beginning to circle, trying to find a place to settle in the trees for the night. As each bird settled on a limb, it would grunt and groan. This kept going on and on and Daniel finally said, "Leonard, remember how Grandfather said cormorants lost their voices, how they started to sound more like pigs than birds? He said that three young women were walking through the woods and they started to bad mouth a bear they met up with."

"Yeah," Leonard said, "and Raven knew that these women were foolish not to respect bears so—"

"So," Daniel said, determined to finish his story, "he turned the women into cormorants and made it so they couldn't sing or call—all they could do was grunt."

Daniel paused. "I guess that was better than getting eaten by the bear."

When they had their fill of eating and talking, the brothers sat quietly for a while, gazing at the sunset. Daniel kept thinking about the white bear, about the way the bear had looked into his eyes, without fear or hesitation. It wasn't just that Daniel had come face to face with the Ghost Bear; it was that the white bear had shared a secret with him. He couldn't put it into words, but he knew that the bear had changed something inside him.

Little by little, he realized, the island was revealing its mysteries to him.

* * *

Settling into their tents for the night, Daniel said sleepily, "Leonard, this was the way it used to be. Before the smallpox."

6
Cedar

While the brothers slept, the clouds moved in. But no rain.

"Before we start exploring, let's get the camp ready in case it rains," Leonard said after breakfast that morning.

Daniel, however, was ready to play. "Oh come on, let's go back into the woods. I really want to see if I can climb one of those monsters," he countered.

Leonard continued his preparation. Finally, with a shrug, Daniel joined him. They rigged up a lean-to with a tarp and driftwood and then moved their gear under it.

Then Leonard said, "I'll bring my climbing equipment. There's no way you can climb one of those cedars without it."

Leonard gathered up his equipment and they headed into the forest. Neither brother actually mentioned the white bear. But the night before they had taken extra precautions, stringing the rope especially high between trees to hang the food out of reach.

And this time in the forest Daniel took a close look at what a bear might eat. At least what a bear might be eating now, before the salmon arrived. As they made their way through the understory following animal trails, Daniel picked berries he knew to be edible, eating the best and depositing the others in his pack. Leonard gave names to the plants Daniel examined. Some were familiar to Daniel, others brand new to him. Orange salmonberries, red and blue huckleberries, shiny red devil's club, dusky blue salal berries, deep red raspberries, purple elderberries, yellow cloudberries, red bearberries, purple crowberries and soft red thimbleberries. And in shades of green—sword ferns taller than the brothers, lacy maidenhair ferns, tiny licorice ferns growing on the trees, cows parsnip, liverwort and moss. Daniel had never seen so much moss, moss draped over tree limbs, carpeting the forest floor, covering rocks and tree trunks—moss everywhere.

They hiked on, quiet now. Then Leonard finally said, as if he knew that Daniel was thinking about the bears, "They have plenty to eat now, but in order to prepare for their winter hibernation, they need the fat and protein that they'll get from the salmon."

"What would happen to the bears if it didn't rain?" Daniel asked.

"Well, you saw what happened when logging destroyed the salmon runs," Leonard said.

Daniel shuddered, remembering the piles of bones on the beach.

"But don't worry; it will rain," Leonard promised.

And of course, they looked for bear signs. This time Daniel listened and watched carefully when Leonard pointed each one out—the shredded trees, the beaten paths through the salal, the tracks and the scat. There were signs everywhere, and not just of bears—of deer, of rabbits, of raccoons, and of foxes. Wait, what were these? They looked closely at tracks that could be those of big dogs, easily twice as big as Daniel's clenched fist. Except that much more likely they were those of...wolves. These tracks were made months ago, when it last rained. They were dried and caked. And they hadn't heard howling the night before, had they? Ahead, some more evidence. Dried scat full of gray rabbit's fur. When Daniel stepped on the scat, all but the fur disintegrated under his shoe. So he stored away in the back of his mind the possibility of meeting up with wolves.

As they hiked along, they listened—to a couple of thrush singing back and forth to each other, to a woodpecker hammering on a snag. After several miles, the lay of the land changed and they started to gain elevation. At the crest of a hill, they came upon a gigantic old cedar, the largest Daniel had ever seen, with an open root cavity at its base. The sides of the cavity were worn and they noticed tufts of fur snagged on the shaggy gray-green cedar bark.

On close examination, Daniel exclaimed, "Some of this fur is brown, and some of it is white! Don't tell me there are brown and white spotted bears on this island!"

Leonard smiled and responded that more likely this was a hibernation den of the white bear and either its brown mother or brown siblings. The brothers talked loud not wanting to surprise another hidden bear, and then Daniel hesitantly peeked inside.

In the musky darkness of the cavity, Daniel thought he saw the bright eyes of a baby bear peeping out at him—but this was just his imagination. There were no fresh signs, no indications that a bear currently inhabited this den.

"Let's try climbing this huge tree, Leonard," Daniel said.

"It would give you quite a view wouldn't it? But I think this tree is too big around, for a start. We'll practice on that one," Leonard said, pointing to a much smaller but still very tall spruce tree nearby. He placed his equipment on the ground to sort it out in preparation for a climb. He had brought his rock climbing gear and was considering how to use it for tree climbing—a couple of heavy ropes, a couple of smaller ones and a harness.

In the meantime, Daniel walked over to the smaller tree, wrapped his arms around it and tried shinnying up using his arms and legs alone. It was a little too big in diameter and he couldn't get a good grip.

"Hey, Leonard, come 'ere for a minute and lean up against this tree."

"Sure, little brother, I guess you can climb on me. But take this skinny rope up there with you and you can set it over a branch on the big cedar," Leonard said, as he handed his brother a coiled rope and a rock.

Leonard leaned against the tree with his arms outstretched, his knees bent. Daniel used his brother's arm for support and his bent leg as a step and hoisted himself up onto Leonard's shoulders. Then he stood up and hooked his arms around the tree. At this height he was able to start his ascent—wrap arms, tighten legs, pull up, wrap, tighten, pull, wrap, tighten, pull. When he reached a good-sized limb, he tried it out for strength and flexibility, something he learned to do from his last failed swinging lesson. When he found that it was sturdy enough to hold his weight, he put his entire body into a "bear hug" around the branch, swung his leg over it and sat up.

"Hey, down there! I'll just hop out on this branch and fly over to the big tree, OK, Leonard?" Daniel boasted to his brother who was looking up at him.

Leonard answered, a little sternly, "Don't be funny. Just take the rope and tie it around the rock and then throw it over the highest branch you can. Do you see one that you can reach?"

"OK, Leonard, I'll do what you say for once," Daniel called down. He took the rock out of his pocket and tied the rope end around it. Spotting a wide and sturdy looking branch high up on the big tree across from him, he aimed the rock. His first throw looked like it would reach the branch, but he hadn't given the rope enough slack. Instead of wrapping around the branch, the rock was stopped in mid-flight and came shooting back down, swinging close to the ground. Leonard had to duck to keep from being hit.

"You missed, little brother!" Leonard yelled. "Next time aim for the branch!"

"Sorry, Leonard," Daniel called down, as he reeled in the rope to try again. This time he made sure the rope had enough slack. When he hurled the rock at the target again, the rope snaked through the air and came to rest dangling over the branch. Then Daniel dropped the other end of the rope down to his brother. From above he watched Leonard use the skinny rope to hoist the two thick ropes up over the branch—one rope for climbing, the other for safety.

"Mission accomplished, Danny, now we can try this cedar. So come on down."

Daniel wanted to keep climbing up the tree but agreed to come down. He used his climbing method in reverse—tighten legs, wrap arms, slide down, tighten, wrap, slide. When he reached the base where it was becoming too wide to grasp, he asked his brother, "Hey, Leonard, come over and be a ladder again, wudja?"

"What's it worth to you?" Leonard asked.

"Nothin'!" Daniel said as he dropped off the tree and landed on his butt on the spongy forest floor.

"Hey, Danny, get up and I'll show you how we'll use the ropes we hung on the tree—this is the climbing rope. We'll take these two small ropes and make prusiks. With a prusik you can climb up the climbing rope. You use the smaller ropes like steps. When you put weight on it, the prusik knot grips the climbing rope; when the weight is off of it, you can easily slide the knot right up the climbing rope. Get the idea?"

"Nope." Daniel was still thinking about his climb rather than paying much attention to his brother's explanation.

"Then I'll show you," Leonard said.

Leonard took the smaller rope and looped it three times around the climbing rope.

Daniel thought it didn't look very difficult to do. "Let me try that, Leonard."

Leonard handed him the two ropes and got him started by holding the climbing rope taut and making a loop with the smaller rope behind it. "Now pull the small rope through the loop."

Daniel did that and was pleased to see the result—a neat coil around the climbing rope.

"OK, now do it again," Leonard said. The second loop got all balled up, so they started again. After two more tries, Daniel got the method down perfectly and was able to make a prusik knot on the second small rope by himself.

"Look how it slides right up the climbing rope, but when you pull down on it, it doesn't budge," Leonard said.

"Yeah, that's cool. Now what?" Daniel asked, feeling impatient to try this out.

"Now take each of the small ropes and make a 'step' at the opposite end, like this." Leonard demonstrated by making a foot-size loop at the end of the smaller rope. Daniel had no trouble completing the second foothold.

"I'll go up first," Leonard said, putting on his harness as if he were putting on a pair of pants. Then he slid his shoes into the footholds. He tied the safety rope off on the base of a nearby tree and handed the other end to Daniel.

"Danny, don't let go of that rope, OK?"

"What's it worth to you?" Daniel countered with a grin.

"So, we're even," Leonard said as he hooked his harness on to the safety rope. Then he started his ascent, alternating his weight on one side and then the other, step, slide, step, slide.

It was slow going in Daniel's estimation, but he admitted to himself that he couldn't do it without ropes. When Leonard made it to the first branch, Daniel was breathing heavily as if he were the one exerting himself.

"Whaddya see, Leonard?" Daniel called up to his brother.

No response.

"Leonard!" Daniel hollered louder.

Still no response.

Minutes passed. Daniel started to pace back and forth, safety rope in hand. "Leonard, I'm gonna let go of the safety rope if you don't tell me what's goin' on up there," Daniel finally said.

This got through to Leonard. "Hold on for a second, wuddja!" Leonard hollered back.

Daniel took a deep breath and looked around. He remembered the den on the other side of the tree. Safety rope in hand, he walked around the massive trunk and sat down at the opening of the hollowed out den. Then he crawled inside. The musky smell and the dampness made him feel that a bear might be back any minute.

Just as he was sticking his head out of the hollow, he heard Leonard shout, "It's raining!"

Daniel looked up. He didn't see any rain drops. Then all of a sudden what seemed like a bucket full of water splashed onto his upturned face, some of it running into his mouth.

Spitting out the earthy tasting water, "Are you sure that's rain, Leonard?" he called back only half joking.

The canopy of the forest had temporarily sheltered the forest floor from the rain by collecting an amazing volume of water in its mass of needles, leaves and branches. Then finally, the rain spilled over.

"Danny, I'm coming down, so hold on to that safety rope," Leonard called out as he began his descent. When his boots dropped to the ground, he was sopping wet but appeared exhilarated.

"That was great! You can try it tomorrow," Leonard said.

"I wanna go up now! I've waited a long time for you. Now I wanna try it," Daniel exclaimed.

"Sorry, Danny, it's raining and it's getting late and we have a long hike back to camp. Aren't you getting hungry? I'm starved!"

"Oh, alright!" Daniel conceded, realizing that he was famished too.

* * *

Hiking back to camp, Leonard told Daniel about what he had seen up in the tree. It wasn't the spectacular view he had expected. Instead, what he saw was right in front of his eyes in the form of a miniature forest. Over the centuries, soil had composted from the needles and leaves that had dropped from the branches above. In it grew tiny trees and ferns and moss and lichen. Leonard described the signs he saw of the creatures that lived there—the insects, the worms, the birds, maybe a vole or even a flying squirrel.

"No wonder the rain didn't taste like rain," Daniel said. Leonard gave his brother a puzzled look.

After a while, they stopped chatting and hiked through the rain in silence, stopping occasionally to pick berries. The forest looked new to Daniel. It was as if it had come into its own. The moss looked more verdant, the berries more luscious, the mushrooms more succulent.

The brothers were sopping wet when they reached their camp, but they found their gear dry under the tarp.

"Hey, Leonard, I forgot we had rigged up this tarp. It's lucky we did," Daniel said, as they stripped off their wet clothes and put on some dry ones.

"Yeah, good timing," Leonard said. "You know, I learned to prepare for rain the hard way. The last camping trip I took, I didn't think about it, and never was able to dry out once the rain started."

Their dinner was simple that night—the last of the dried meats and fish they had bought in Stewart's Landing, one of the packets of dried soup, the berries they had gathered. Leonard mentioned their food wouldn't last as long as he had thought. If they were to stay any longer, they would have to rely more on the forest and the sea.

* * *

As they fell asleep listening to the raindrops falling on the tarp, Daniel pictured a river of salmon in the sea, swimming steadily toward the mouth of their island stream.

7
Salmon

It rained hard all night. By morning the clouds hung low and the air was heavy with moisture, but the rain had let up. The brothers were awakened by the sound of a raven's call from a high perch in the forest. The bird's "Quok! Quok! Quok!" sounded like a grand announcement and Daniel thought, "I wonder if the salmon are home?"

Mixing biscuits while watching his older brother light the campstove, Daniel said, "Hey, Leonard, wouldn't it be nice to have some salmon to go along with the biscuits and berries?"

"It sure would. Especially since we're getting low on food," Leonard answered. "You know, Danny, we're going to have to head back in a few days. And anyway, you've got to get back for school."

Daniel's face darkened. "I don't want to go back to school. There's no reason to."

Leonard hesitated a moment before he replied, "I felt the same way at your age. When I left home, I was 16. That was way too young. If I hadn't met up with Charlie Amber, I probably would still be living on the streets. Or dead."

Daniel said, "But you wouldn't be an artist now if you didn't leave home."

"Maybe not, but I would never have accomplished anything if I hadn't gone back to school. So," Leonard said, "you think we can catch some salmon? I brought a fishing net."

"I want to try a spear! Grandfather said he learned how from Great-Great Grandfather. All you need are some sticks. We'll catch a bunch of salmon. Then we'll have plenty of food and we can stay a while longer, right?" Daniel asked.

"I guess so, Danny," Leonard said. "But let's not get our hopes up. The salmon may not be here."

"Let's go to the stream as soon as we finish breakfast," Daniel said.

Leonard took the bowl of biscuit batter from Daniel and poured it into a pan he had heated up on the burner.

"Sure you wouldn't rather go back to the big cedar and take your turn climbing?" Leonard asked.

"Well, I want to, but that can wait 'til after we catch the salmon," Daniel concluded.

It started raining again just as the brothers began hiking down the beach toward the stream. The calm sea they were accustomed to was gone. Now the sea was unsettled. Wind was whipping the surface into little whitecaps, and waves restlessly slapped the shore. But today the brothers were prepared for the weather. Leonard knew they were coming into the rainy season, so he had brought plenty of raingear. In their yellow rain jackets, floppy rimmed hats and rubber boots, they looked like fishermen. Except that they had no fishing boat and no gear. They were going to see whether the salmon were running and what it would take to catch one. They would see whether Daniel was right that all they needed was a stick.

Pointing out to sea, Daniel said, "Look Leonard, can you see the salmon heading in?"

Squinting through the drizzle, they examined the white disturbances in the water. No, they concluded, just little whitecaps.

The brothers weren't the only ones anticipating the event. The familiar round heads of seals were bobbing in the water. And much larger sea lions were barking with impatience. As the brothers approached the stream, they spotted four eagles circling high overhead and a number of others on watch in the treetops. A gang of gulls was fighting over airspace lower down. Crows, ravens, an osprey and even a couple of vultures were cruising back and forth.

The brothers scrambled up on a large boulder overlooking the stream. Daniel was happy to see that where there had been a tiny trickle, there was now a torrent of white water. Where there had been a dry rock face with a darkened watermark, there was now a respectable waterfall. The stream was ready for the salmon. They settled in for the wait.

After a while, Daniel yelled over the roar of the water, "Leonard, do you think the bears are watching for the salmon too?"

Leonard didn't have time to answer.

A white bear sprang into the stream from his post in a tree behind them. With a big splash, the bear hit the water and then hopped up onto a rock not five feet away from them and peered into a pool below. At the same time, a salmon came arching and spiraling over the whitewater, landing in the quiet pool beneath the bear.

It must have been this salmon that had been the white bear's call to action, Daniel speculated, but how had the white bear known before any of the other creatures? Was it the salmon's smell that only the bear could perceive?

Now the iridescent silver and red salmon was swimming slowly in a circle, its dorsal fin and part of its body exposed above the surface of the water. It looked like it was resting before it would attempt to scale the waterfall, its final challenge. But the white bear was balanced on a rock above the pool. This bear might present the salmon's most formidable obstacle yet.

The brothers had a ringside seat to watch this contest. Daniel figured the stakes were high.

He knew that for the salmon, it would mean completing its life's mission, its long journey, by spawning where it was hatched. Since it left the stream a few years before, the salmon would have traveled many miles. *Even thousands?* he wondered. It would have avoided death innumerable times—death in the jaws of whales and sea lions, or the beaks of eagles and osprey, or the hooks and nets of fishermen. Somehow the salmon knew when to return. And somehow it knew where.

As for the white bear, Daniel was well aware of the stakes—catch salmon or eventually die of starvation. He thought back at the bones they had found on the beach of his Great-Great Grandmother's island and remembered Leonard's words. Salmon would satisfy a summer-long craving that would prepare him for his winter's hibernation. This would be the bear's first meal of protein and fat since the spring salmon season ended. Although the fruits of the forest sustained him for the summer, the white bear needed to gain a hundred or more pounds from the salmon to survive the winter. He would need to consume many salmon before the fall spawning season was over. This salmon would be his first.

The white bear sprawled out on the boulder. He hung his head over the water and reached down into the pool with his paw, claws extended in order to snag the fish. Because the pool was confined and in easy reach of the bear, it looked like the contest would be over quickly. The first fish would be the white bear's first feast. The bear's outstretched paw began tracking the salmon around the pool, and at each turn the bear got closer to the prize. Daniel's gaze followed the salmon around and around the pool, his body tense with expectation.

Just as the salmon was about to be snagged, Daniel glimpsed a huge dark mass hurtling past. This time not only were the brothers stunned but so was the white bear. A black bear had sprung from the very same perch that the white bear had used earlier. In jumping into the stream the black bear pushed the white bear off the rock he was fishing from. The two bears both ended up in the pool with the salmon.

Now it looked like the contest would be between the two bears, and from the looks of it, not necessarily a peaceful one. Both bears stood upright on their hind legs and faced each other. Mouths open and incisors bared, their faces were close enough to the other that the vapor from their breath mingled in the chilled air. The way they stepped around each other and held their forepaws like fists, they looked to Daniel like two heavyweight boxers positioning themselves before the fight.

The salmon seized the moment and accelerated its swim. Then it leaped triumphantly through the air and disappeared above the waterfall. Both bears spun around, but it was too late.

After that, the two bears wasted no more time. Their attention turned to the mouth of the stream. Daniel followed their gaze. He saw a multitude of small disturbances in the water going against the flow. The salmon were running. Thousands of them.

What followed was a festival of feeding, not only for the two bears, but also for other bears and for eagles, osprey, sea lions and seals. Gulls, vultures and ravens were circling overhead, ready to take advantage of any leftovers. Raccoons and foxes waited in the woods for their portions. The brothers were the only spectators at this feast.

Daniel had never seen such a feast. After a few hours, the stream had turned a blood red. It was roiling with fish. And salmon continued to come. Many made it up the waterfall. Many became a meal for the bears. Sometimes a bear would steal away into the woods with a salmon. When the bear had eaten the best parts, the fatty skin and the heart, he left the flesh for other forest creatures. The scavengers came last and cleaned up the carcass.

After watching this revelry into the afternoon, the brothers could no longer ignore their own hunger. Leonard got up first and Daniel followed. They left their observation post without any of the revelers taking notice.

As soon as they had put some distance between themselves and the commotion at the stream, Daniel chattered excitedly. "That was the same white bear we met in the forest, wasn't it Leonard! I can't believe those two bears let that salmon win! Leonard, I'm starving!"

Leonard asked with a smile, "Danny, what would you like for lunch?"

"Well, let's see. How about oatmeal with raisins? Or maybe some dried soup? Come on, Leonard, I can't believe with all that salmon, we're comin' back with nothin'!"

Leonard was also animated. "But, Danny, did you ever imagine you would be right in the middle of feeding bears? I kept thinking we should be afraid. But we weren't! It just seemed so normal to be there watching it all!"

"I know," Daniel said quietly, reflecting on all that had happened. After they walked silently for a few minutes, he said, "I still wanna catch a salmon, but I guess I can wait 'til tomorrow."

* * *

Back at camp, they went about the motions of cooking their meal, but their minds were still at the stream. It was only late afternoon when they finished eating and cleaning up, but they felt exhausted and a bit dazed. They decided that they would climb into their sleeping bags under the tarp and just rest.

Daniel said, "That was so cool the way they stood up on their hind legs. Do you think the white bear and the black bear were going to fight? Do you think they knew each other?"

Leonard answered, "You know, Danny, I'm still having a hard time believing we were able to sit there with all that feeding going on and not disturb the animals. My guess is that the white bear and the black bear are used to each other, maybe they are even siblings. It was more posturing than anything."

"But it lost them the first salmon, didn't it?" Daniel said. "Do you think the bears will let us fish with them tomorrow? They wouldn't attack us because we're trying to take their salmon, would they? Grandfather and Mother said you'd better not offend the Salmon People if you wanted to get any fish. I don't think we did anything like that, do you?"

"No, I don't think so," Leonard said. "If we ever catch a salmon we'll do what Mother always did. She would always toss all the remains of the first salmon, the bones and the skin, even the head, into the fire. Then she would drink some fresh water. She said that way, the salmon would be able to go home to their Village Under the Sea. Then they'd become Salmon People again and return to the river as salmon in a few years. As a favor to the People. I guess, we'll just have to see what happens when we try to fish. It won't be easy to spear a fish, but I don't think the bears will pay any more attention to us than they did today."

* * *

The brothers chatted into the night, the pounding downpour reminding them that the salmon would continue running. Just as they were falling asleep, they heard the howling of wind. *Or,* Daniel thought, *wolves?*

8
Wolf

Wolves. The moment Daniel woke up the next morning he thought about the sound he had heard before going to sleep the night before. He couldn't get it out of his mind all throughout breakfast.

"Hey, Leonard, did you hear howling last night?" he asked, trying to sound casual.

Leonard replied, "Yeah, the wind was pretty fierce. It's not bad right now but the weather's not over. I think we're in for a big storm."

"This time I'm gonna be ready. I'm gonna make some spears before we head over to the stream," Daniel said, not concerned at all about the weather.

Daniel started down the beach looking for some sticks of wood he could fashion into spears. He found a long narrow piece of driftwood that already had the rough shape of a spear. All he needed to do was sharpen one end. He could do that when he got back to camp. Now he needed just one more, for Leonard, so that they both could fish at the same time.

He jerked his head around, eyes scouring the forest. No, nothing moving, except some crows shaking branches as they dashed in and out of the woods. Had he heard another howl, or was he just a little jumpy from waking up thinking about wolves? He wasn't sure.

Daniel had never actually seen or heard a wolf in real life before. As a child, he heard plenty of stories about wolves. And when the villagers in the wolf clan danced and howled like a pack of wolves, he had been enthralled though a little scared. Sometimes people said they were back, but it always turned out to be coyotes. Daniel knew the wolves had been hunted down long before.

Maybe, he thought, his nerves were on edge because of his itch to catch a salmon.

Soon he found another piece of driftwood that he thought would work as a spear. With a "spear" in each hand, he hurried back up the beach toward camp, surveying the forest for any sign of movement as he went.

"Hey, Leonard, I found us some fishing poles," Daniel announced when he reached camp, relieved to be back with his brother.

"Good, let me get my carving knife out. We'll see if we can make ourselves some spears and do our ancestors proud," Leonard said, as he finished stowing their cooking equipment. He went into his pack and pulled out a large carving knife sheathed in rawhide.

"I used this knife to work on the dugout canoe with Charlie Amber," Leonard said, handing the hefty knife to Daniel.

Daniel unloosened the leather tie, grasped the cool abalone handle, and unsheathed the knife. He gently touched the sharp edge of the blade and then ran his finger along the shiny flat metal surface.

Picking up one of the driftwood poles, Daniel said, "This'll work, no problem."

He sat down on a driftwood log and started whittling the end of the pole, with sure strokes directed away from his body, finding the knife slicing through the wood without much effort. It felt satisfying to have Leonard watch him do this job. Daniel knew he did it well. He had learned all that Grandfather could teach him and practiced whenever he got a chance. Now was his opportunity to show Leonard what he had accomplished.

As he whittled there on the beach with Leonard sitting next to him, he suddenly thought he could smell the salmon Mother used to cook. An image of her standing at the stove when he came home from school one fall day popped into his mind. He remembered asking her if he could go down to the beach while dinner was cooking. When he turned to look back, he could see her smiling through the kitchen window of the doublewide, her kind eyes telling him he was everything to her. Just as he was doing now, he sat on a driftwood log and carved. Only then, the aroma of baking salmon drew him back to his house to feast with Mother and Grandfather.

Looking up from his carving, he was struck by how much Leonard's eyes looked like Mother's. "Leonard, I'm sure we're going to have some luck today."

With the whittling finished, they took their spears and

headed down the beach to the mouth of the stream. Even though the rain had stopped, they were wearing the same raingear that had kept them dry the day before. Looking out at the darkening clouds gathering over the water, Daniel thought, *Maybe Leonard was right, the howling was just the wind. Maybe a big storm's on its way.*

Even from a distance, they could see and hear that the activity around the stream hadn't decreased. In fact maybe there were even more birds and animals congregated than the day before. Only one thing was different. Above the din at the stream, the brothers heard howling coming from the forest. And the wind hadn't started up yet.

They glanced at each other nervously and slowed up their pace. Nothing needed to be said for it to be clear that the howling was not the wind. Their eyes searched the woods as they drew near the stream.

When they reached the stream, it looked like the morning after a wild party, with salmon bones and skin strewn all over the rocks. And it appeared some of the partygoers didn't know when to call it quits—gulls, ravens, crows, eagles, hawks and osprey still formed a raucous mob above the stream. And the stream itself was still bubbling with the slithering silver bodies of salmon. But no bears—or wolves—were in sight.

Daniel climbed up to the same boulder where the white bear had been the day before. Leonard lagged behind.

Remembering the black bear's ambush, Daniel cautioned, "Hey, Leonard, watch for bears while I try catching a fish. They're swimming slow in this pool." Leonard had already begun his watch.

Daniel positioned himself on the boulder, lifted his spear above his head, just as Grandfather had described, took aim and let it fly. His aim was good and it entered the water in the exact path where the salmon was heading. But the salmon sensed the disturbance and made an about face just in time. Daniel was not deterred. He reached into the water and retrieved his spear. This time he crouched down on the boulder and tensed up to give the spear more speed. He aimed at the other fish. The same thing happened. Now the salmon were circling the pool faster than before. He would have to wait until they settled down or until a new group entered. As he sat waiting, the two salmon repeated the first salmon's feat of the day before—accelerating, then leaping out of the water with an unmatched determination. Their bodies twisted and turned as they scaled the falls in unison. Daniel began to consider whether the salmon's desire to return home was stronger than his desire to catch a fish.

Waiting for his next opportunity, he heard, over the roar of the stream, faint howls echoing from the forest. He turned his head to look at Leonard. Leonard was straining to hear it better. The howling got louder.

Leonard hopped up on the boulder to join his brother. The atmosphere was electrified. Every muscle in their bodies taut, the brothers watched for any movement. Then, on the far side of the stream, like a phantom, a black wolf emerged from the forest. It was dusky black not gray. The shadowy creature floated closer, head lowered but penetrating yellow eyes fixed on them. The wolf paused, stared warily at them for a few seconds and then turned around and disappeared back into the darkness.

The brothers glanced at each other as if needing confirmation that what they had seen was not an apparition. Whatever it was, they had both seen it. Daniel then remembered his mission to catch a salmon. But what if the wolf returned? What if another wolf was watching from behind them in the forest? Finally, it didn't matter—his unfulfilled desire to catch that salmon outweighed everything else, and he picked up his spear and aimed it at a salmon swimming slowly around the perimeter of the pool.

Then in a repeat performance, the white bear appeared out of nowhere and landed in the pool where Daniel's spear was pointed. Daniel dropped his spear in surprise. The bear was seemingly oblivious to the brothers, as he had been the day before. But his fishing technique was definitely improved. Now the bear submerged his head into the water and a moment later came up with a wriggling salmon in his mouth. He hopped up on a rock and bit into the salmon—he ate only the heart and left the rest on the rocks. Immediately, an eagle swooped down. Daniel could feel the cyclone of moving air the eagle's wings whipped up. Daniel watched the eagle rip off a chunk of red flesh and take flight with it dangling from his yellow beak.

The white bear was already snagging another fish. This time he ran into the woods with it and reappeared a few moments later, salmon blood smeared all over his white fur. Some yelps followed by high-pitched howls drifted from the darkness where the white bear had left the remains of this last catch. It occurred to Daniel that the black wolf they had seen earlier might actually be a mother. He imagined her chewing the fish the bear had deposited, then regurgitating it for her pups to scrap over, just as he had once witnessed a coyote mother do back home. Daniel wondered whether the family was accustomed to getting their share of the feast in this way.

The white bear continued his haul. He snagged the next salmon and then, inexplicably, he shook his head and tossed it in Daniel's direction. Daniel held out his hands and caught the salmon as if responding to the bear hollering, "Heads up! Here it comes!" Holding a twenty-pound salmon, Daniel stood for a moment stunned. Then he pinned the struggling salmon on the boulder with his hands while Leonard picked up the spear and stabbed the fish under the gills. They operated as if this was something they had done many times before.

Heading back to camp, Daniel cradled the salmon in his arms. Leonard carried a spear in each hand. *How did I catch that salmon?* Daniel mused. But then, he thought, how could it be otherwise in a place where a black bear was white and a gray wolf black? And where the bear shared their catch with the eagles and the wolves?

* * *

To Daniel, the first fish smelled unbelievably good as it roasted over a fire on the beach. While Leonard cooked, he sat on a log and traced shapes in the sand with a stick.

"Hey, Leonard, why did you leave home?" he asked, gazing at the lines he was making.

Leonard looked up, a little surprised. "You mean, after Mother died?"

"No, I mean, when you were 16."

"Hmm, I guess I wanted to see if I could make it on my own," he replied, as he poked the salmon with a stick to see if it was flaky and fully cooked. "And, when I left, Father was laid off. I guess I didn't want to end up being a logger like him."

"How did you find Charlie Amber?" Daniel asked.

"He found me. I was trying to sell a woodcarving at a gift shop in Seattle and Charlie walked in and asked where I was from. Turns out he's from a village on the river up north of our island. He said he needed help with the totem pole he was carving at a cultural center. I went with him and started working with him."

"Why did you go back to school?"

"That was Charlie's idea. I did it because he wanted me to. It went pretty well until the day Charlie told me that they called to say that Father had been killed in that logging accident. Then I just lost it. I didn't go to school, instead I went back to the streets where Charlie first found me."

"But you ended up going back to school."

"Well, Charlie found me and sent me home to Grandfather and Mother. You were a toddler. Other than play with you, I didn't want to do anything. Finally, Grandfather told me I should go back to Charlie. So I did. That time I stayed in school and worked hard." Testing the salmon again, he said, "Hey, let's dig in."

When they finished eating, the brothers took all the skin and bones, every bit that remained of the salmon, even the head and tail, and threw it into the fire, just as Mother had always done. Then they drank some fresh water.

After cleaning up, Daniel walked down to the seashore by himself. The tide was going out and the sun was getting low on the horizon, casting an orange glow on the water. A raven stood next to him and made soft clucking sounds. Daniel picked up a giant kelp bulb, swung the long stem around and around over his head and then flung it as far as he could into the sea. Watching it drift out to sea on the tide, a dam of sadness suddenly broke open in Daniel and tears flowed down his cheeks into his mouth. He felt as if he were gulping salty seawater. An image flooded his mind of salmon returning through an undersea passage to the Village of the Salmon People. He thought of Mother and somehow he knew that she was smiling at the way they took care of the salmon and sent it back home.

Inhaling in little spasms and feeling sleepy now, Daniel

wiped his face with his two hands and made his way back up the beach to the campfire.

* * *

That night Daniel had a dream that a raven, carrying a ball of fire in his beak, flew him home to Grandfather.

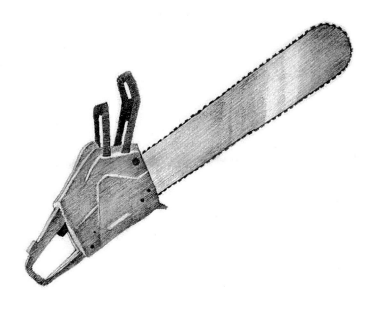

9
Chainsaw

Daniel and Leonard were strolling through the forest in a light rain after their breakfast of salmon, berries and biscuits. They were heading for the big cedar. While cleaning up after breakfast, they had again discussed whether to go back to the stream to fish for more salmon or whether to hike to the big tree for Daniel's turn at a climb. This time Daniel opted for the climb. With his fill of salmon, the challenge of climbing one of those cedars had come back to him in full force. Leonard said he was happy to go either way. So they set off into the forest.

The animals alerted the brothers first. In an instant, the forest was still—no chirping of songbirds, no hammering of woodpeckers, no calling of ravens. The chipmunks stopped dead in their tracks. All was quiet except for the sound of the chainsaws far off in the distance. Then it seemed that every animal began to dart about and to make distress sounds.

Daniel had an immediate and sickening realization of what it meant. It meant the end for this place where he had swum with a seal, and climbed with a bear. Where he had shared a bear's haul of salmon with an eagle and a wolf. This place where trees grew so big that they were like silent monsters stalking the earth and where the forest canopy was a miniature world of its own. And maybe it meant the end for the Ghost Bear.

The brothers moved in the direction of that dreaded sound. After hours of running and stumbling through the underbrush, they crested the hill where the big cedar stood.

Quiet again. Then as if an earthquake had hit, the ground began to shake as an 800-year-old cedar splintered, and crashed violently onto the forest floor. The giant lay slain. It was not their big cedar that had been felled but that was no consolation to Daniel. The tree was equally stupendous. They stood on the hill watching the scene as if it were a horror movie. Nothing had been left undisturbed. For a few moments the surrounding earth, plants and trees whirled around in unnaturally slow motion.

When the dust settled, the loggers, big beefy men with massive arms and oversized bellies, ogled their victim. Daniel and Leonard ducked down and watched, unseen.

"That monster should bring us twenty grand, clear, huh, Pa?" the younger man gloated. Daniel could hear every word in the morbidly quiet forest. It didn't seem right to him that these accomplices might be father and son, although when he looked again he could see a resemblance. To Daniel, the older one looked like a meaner and grayer version of the younger.

"That ain't nothin'. There are plenty more big ones in this no-man's land. Those Injun's don't even know the money they're sittin' on," the older one growled.

"Ha! By the time they figur' it out, it'll all be gone!" the younger man said.

The brothers listened to this exchange until the loggers picked up their saws again and started scoping out another victim. Then Daniel and Leonard crept away until they were no longer within hearing distance.

Daniel spoke in a whisper but with conviction, "Leonard, we've gotta stop 'em!"

"I know Danny, these aren't even loggers—they're just poachers, they're thieves! They think they can get away with stealing these trees because they don't think anyone's gonna know."

"So what do we do, Leonard?" As Daniel asked this question, he remembered the picture he had seen of a young woman sitting on a platform in a gigantic tree, with an angry logger holding a chainsaw up against the tree. The caption was something like, "Young woman saves big tree." That was back in Seattle when Leonard had gotten him out of the detention center and he was feeling humiliated and angry. The picture of this woman stuck in his mind. He thought he knew how she felt. And for a moment the fear he imagined she had felt swept over him.

Leonard said, "The only thing we can do is get back to Stewart's Landing as fast as possible and call the tribal police. Let's get packing."

"No! Leonard, I can't leave this place! They're gonna see the big cedar and cut it before anyone gets back," Daniel argued.

"There's nothing we can do to stop them without help,

Danny. Those guys are tough and they won't stop at anything to get the money they want."

"I'm going to sit in the big cedar until you get back. They won't cut the tree with me in it."

"That's crazy, Danny! I can't let you do that. You could get killed," Leonard replied almost frantically. Then he added sternly, "NO! Let's get going."

In the drizzling rain, Daniel hung back a little on their return to camp. He was deep in thought. Grandfather's story had said that the Ghost Bear should always be left in peace, he thought. Now those thieves were out to destroy the island—the white bear would die just like the bears on Great-Great Grandmother's island. It would be just how Leonard had described. First the streams would get warm and muddy, then the salmon would stop coming back. Without salmon, the white bear and most of the other animals would eventually starve. No, he couldn't let this happen. It was up to him. Leonard would go back to get the tribal police, but he had to save the big cedar.

No matter how scared he was. No matter what happened.

When they arrived back at camp, Daniel turned to Leonard, squared his shoulders and folded his arms across his chest. He declared, "Leonard, I've decided—I'm not leaving."

Leonard was about to object when he looked into Daniel's eyes. Instead he asked, "Did you mean you want to set up a platform in the big cedar and tree-sit, like a protester?"

"Yeah, like the woman in the newspaper," Daniel replied.

"Danny, she did that with a whole group of protesters behind her. And the people she was up against were loggers not poachers. These guys would sooner shoot you than let you stop them."

"They won't shoot a kid," Daniel replied with a confidence that surprised even him. Then he thought, *We didn't actually see a gun, did we?* But he stopped himself from following this train of thought and said, "So here's what we need to do. First, we gather wood to build the platform, then we do some more fishing. We need salmon for both of us. How long will it take you to get back to Stewart's Landing?"

Leonard went along with the planning, although he sounded uneasy. "If I go up north to Hannah Island instead of back to Stewart's Landing, it'll take four days. Then it'll take another couple of days for Grandfather and the police to get a motorboat ready and for us to get back here. So six days, best case. You know what the weather's starting to look like. A storm could slow this whole thing down."

"But it could also keep the poachers from getting much done, too."

At the mention of Grandfather, Daniel thought about how much he'd like to see him, but then he put that thought aside and said, "So you'll need maybe six or seven day's worth of food and I'll need more than a week. We'd better get fishin'. Do you have that net?"

Leonard was already heading down to the canoe. "Danny, there's some driftwood planks down here. We could use them to build the platform."

"So, I'll get the wood and you get us ready for fishing," Daniel said, in his new take-charge manner.

As he set off down the beach, Daniel glanced back at his brother taking the fishing gear out of the canoe. He wished he and Leonard could just paddle away from the poachers. But he knew he could never leave this island now that it was threatened. He started looking around for driftwood they could use to build the platform. How strange, he thought, that he was looking for material to build his home up in a tree. He hadn't even had a chance to climb it yet. Now he was wondering whether he'd be able to save it from the poachers. He picked up a weathered board and held it upright, measuring it against his own height. It was a little shorter than he was, and his feet would dangle over the edge when he tried to sleep, but it would do. He then found two other boards of an equivalent size. After he lugged the boards up to the campsite, he found Leonard waiting for him, fishing net and spear in hand.

Leonard shook his head and said, "I must be crazy to let you do this," he said. Then he added, "OK, let's do some fishin'."

Nothing at the stream had changed—except the way Daniel felt. It was still churning with salmon and the birds and animals were still creating a commotion. But Daniel felt like he was no longer a part of it. The poachers had changed all that. Now his role was to protect these animals from people, people who were greedy and stupid, but still they were people. This new role weighed heavily on him. Yet, it kept him focused.

As they drew near the stream, Daniel said, "Leonard, you do the fishing. You're better at it and we need to get going."

Leonard took a stance over the same pool, now deserted by the bears. He dipped his net into the pool and held it still. When the next salmon entered the pool, it swam right into the net. Leonard easily yanked the net up and plopped the fish on the boulder. Daniel speared the fish under the gills. With this method, they quickly caught three more fish and headed back to camp carrying a fish in each hand.

Leonard started a fire as soon as they got back to camp. The salmon would have to roast for as long as possible in order to dry out enough to last for a week. Daniel worked on gathering and packing the equipment they would need to construct a platform high up in the big cedar. Again he thought about how he hadn't even had time to practice climbing with ropes, but he tried to keep his mind on the task. What would he need? Leonard's climbing equipment, fresh water in bottles, food for a week, a flashlight, matches, a knife, raingear, clothes, plastic bags, sleeping bag, tarp. He patted his pocket to feel for the little carving knife Leonard had given him that belonged to Father.

After the salmon had roasted, Daniel and Leonard sat down for their last meal together at the campsite. It was late afternoon and they would have to start their hike into the forest as soon as they ate. If they were going to build a platform without encountering the poachers, they would have to do it at dawn before the poachers had time to reach the big cedar. That meant hiking for several hours in the evening carrying their large load and camping that night in the forest near the big cedar.

The brothers were subdued as they sat around the campfire thinking about what lay ahead. Daniel forced himself to eat more than he wanted and then quickly went about the business at hand, cleaning up the camp and finishing the packing.

When they were ready to leave, backpacks stuffed with gear, they positioned themselves at either end of the stack of planks that Leonard had lashed together to make them easier to carry. When they lifted the heavy boards up, Daniel remembered how uncertain he had felt when he picked up his end of the canoe at Stewart's Landing, just a short time ago. This time he knew he could pull his weight. He was sure now that Leonard trusted him. After all, Leonard was leaving him on the island alone, to face whatever there was to face.

With a glance over his shoulder at the canoe nestled between driftwood logs on the beach, Daniel turned back to Leonard and said, "I'm ready. Let's go."

10
Raven

A raven's "Quok!" woke up the sleeping forest just before dawn. Daniel was disoriented for a few moments and then he remembered what he had to do. His stomach felt like it was tying itself in a prusik knot.

"That raven woke us up just in time, Danny," Leonard said, trying to act cheerful. "Have some biscuits and we can get to work."

After one dry bite of biscuit, Daniel stood up and said, "Let's get started building the platform."

"The first thing we need to do is set the ropes in the branch of the big cedar just like we did before," Leonard said.

Leonard planted himself against the smaller spruce tree

next to the big cedar so Daniel could hop up on his shoulders. In a flash, Daniel was sitting on a branch in the tree. He breathed in the cool moist air, saw the filtered sunbeams, and listened to the birds greet the morning. This calmed him. With a steady arm he tossed a line, tied around a rock, high into the air. The rock went over a branch of the big cedar and carried the line with it. While Leonard got three ropes set over the branch—a safety rope, a climbing rope and one additional rope for hauling—Daniel climbed down and jumped nimbly to the forest floor.

Leonard was busy lashing the hauling rope to one of the boards. "Danny, I'll climb up the big cedar and then you pull on one end of the hauling rope to raise the boards, one by one. I'll help from above. When I was up there the last time I found the perfect place for a platform. There's another branch at the same height right next to the one the ropes are set on. Once I lash the boards together, the platform will sit securely on those two huge branches. It'll be almost like standing on solid ground up there, the branches are so massive. Then all we need to do is secure the platform from some upper branches to keep it from going anywhere in a high wind. With your weight on it, it won't fall."

He added with a smile, "It might swing a little but it won't fall."

Just as he had done the first time he had climbed the tree, Leonard put on his harness, cinched it to the safety rope, and slid his boots into the footholds. Handing the end of the safety rope to Daniel, he said, "Once I'm up there, I'll tell you when to start hauling." Then he started his ascent, alternating his weight on one prusik then the other, step, slide, step, slide.

Daniel watched his brother gain altitude, imagining what it would be like when he finally got his turn to climb.

It'll seem like a one-way ticket, he thought, *at least for a while.* When Leonard finally reached the branch, he disappeared from sight. Daniel nervously looked around, remembering that the poachers might be headed their way any time now. Then Leonard called down to Daniel to start pulling on the hauling rope. One of the boards began to lift and twist around as it ascended. It wasn't long before all three boards were up in the tree and Daniel was left waiting at the foot of the tree for Leonard to finish his building.

Daniel had the urge to take a peek into the hibernation den on the other side of the tree. Still holding onto the safety rope he walked around the giant tree and crawled into the den. He wondered if the white bear would use it this season. His mind drifted back to his first encounter with the white bear in the forest. He smiled recalling the way the bear had looked at him.

Then he thought of the poachers and was jolted back to the present. *I'd better get out of here in case Leonard is ready to come down.*

When Daniel crawled out of the den, Leonard was already calling to him, "Hey, Danny, I'm coming down."

It was finally time for Daniel to climb the big cedar. He pulled Leonard's harness over his jeans, slid his tennis shoes into the footholds, cinched himself onto the safety rope and started his ascent. It seemed slow having to step and slide, step and slide, alternately putting weight on one prusik while he slid the other up the climbing rope. This was much slower than his ropeless method of climbing. But he couldn't even see around the wall of cedar in front of him and he knew that without this equipment he would never be able to reach the branch a hundred feet above him.

Once Daniel got into the rhythm of the climb, he began to feel the freedom that always accompanied leaving the ground. His body felt light, his mind clear. When he looked down, Leonard was beginning to look small and far off. When he looked up, massive branches formed a great ceiling above him. He could see the ropes that Leonard had wrapped securely around them to hold the platform in place. Finally, Daniel reached the place, not even halfway up the gigantic tree, where he'd be spending a week, if all went well. He pulled himself up onto the platform and stood up. It felt solid, just as Leonard said it would.

The first thing Daniel viewed was a raven out on a limb above the platform. The bird looked huge amid the miniature forest world that Leonard had described—tiny trees, ferns, salal, lichens, mushrooms, growing in the humus deposited over centuries. Daniel was sure that he'd see signs of the other little animals that Leonard mentioned, as soon as he got a chance to look. Now, though, he needed to haul up the rest of his gear and then say good-bye to Leonard. When he reeled in the ropes that Leonard had been holding, he realized that his connection to his brother, and to the solid ground, was being severed.

For how long? he mused.

"Danny, I'll be back here with Grandfather soon!" Leonard called as he slowly moved away from the tree, walking backwards, still looking up at Daniel.

Looking down at his brother, Daniel felt a twinge of regret. He wished he hadn't thrown that rock and made a gash in Leonard's canoe. He wished he had told Leonard how much he had learned from him, how important Leonard's faith in him was. He saw it all in a flash. He saw himself in Seattle, trying hard to impress his brother for reasons that no longer mattered. And he saw himself now, willing to risk everything to save what he cared about—the white bear, the salmon, the cedars, all the other animals and plants—the island itself.

Then Daniel became aware that Leonard hesitated. "Go on, Leonard, you know where to find me!" He watched Leonard disappear into the forest.

There was no time to be sad. It was now raining so hard that by the time Daniel rigged up the tarp, a heavy stream of rain was pouring from the roof where it sagged a little. He was about to tighten the line to make the tarp lie flatter when he realized that this was how he could replenish his water supply. He took two empty bottles out of his pack and placed one under the spout. It was soon filled. He had brought enough food and water for a week's stay up in the tree, but more water might come in handy. His next task was to arrange his gear on the small platform so that he could move around and sleep, as well as prepare food. He hung his two smoked salmon from the tree under the tarp so they would stay dry. Along with the berries the brothers had picked and some crackers they had brought, this would be all there was to eat for a week.

With his chores complete, he sat down under the tarp and looked around. A raven was peering at him from a perch nearby, tilting his shiny head back and forth and making little tapping sounds with his beak. Daniel imagined him trying to mouth the words, "Why are you up here? What happened to your wings?"

Though glad he had a neighbor, Daniel was too hungry to take the time to get to know him. He took one of the salmon down from the tree and cut off a chunk. The familiar flavor made him think of the salmon stream. Were the salmon still running? What about next year? Would there be a clear cold stream to come back to? For today, it looked like the poachers might not be back. Maybe the heavy rain kept them away. But they would be back. Of that Daniel was sure.

A knocking sound snapped Daniel back to the present. It was his raven neighbor. In reply, Daniel put his tongue on the roof of his mouth, and clicked back at the raven. Then the raven made an even louder knocking sound that made him jump. And smile. Daniel finally addressed the big bird, at least three times as large as a crow, standing before him. "Grandfather told me lots of stories about you, Raven. He said you're the Trickster. Would you like to hear one of them?" When Raven cocked his head and preened, Daniel continued.

"So there you were at the beginning of the world. You cracked open a huge shell on the beach with your big beak. You watched the first guy poke his hand out of the shell. That guy really liked the feel of the air and the rain. But when you had fun was when the second guy stuck his bare bottom out of the shell. You pecked at him! Right where it hurts!" Daniel grinned as he remembered dancing the Cocky Raven's dance alongside Grandfather, clicking and cackling at the predicament of these first humans.

As he talked to Raven, he found that the bird's responses were becoming more and more like talking. There were so many variations on the "quok" sound—"quaaks," "queeks" and "quooks." Raven's finale as he flew off sounded like a drum roll and left Daniel chuckling.

That evening, the first up in the tree alone, Daniel felt pangs of loneliness, wishing he were back with Grandfather. How he could ever have been so anxious to leave home? How could he have been worried about talking to Grandfather about what happened in Seattle?

He thought about how, when he was a little boy, Grandfather's stories had made him feel as if he were there. He would sit on Grandfather's lap next to the fire listening to all the stories, imagining so vividly the scenes that Grandfather described that later it was hard to remember what he actually saw and what he only imagined. He remembered seeing Raven fly over an island where no people ever walked. And he could swear he watched Raven flying through the forest between the huge cedars. And didn't he feel the breeze from Raven's wings as he flew over a sleeping black bear and turned him white? Definitely, he heard Raven's call. Those images from his childhood began to mix with his recent memories of the animals here on the island.

Then, hearing a "quok!" as Raven flew off into the growing darkness, a thought occurred to Daniel. Maybe Raven's call wasn't a promise of peace, maybe it was a warning.

Of what? he pondered.

Beginning to shiver, he pulled his sweatshirt hood over his head, hunkered down in his sleeping bag, and fell asleep.

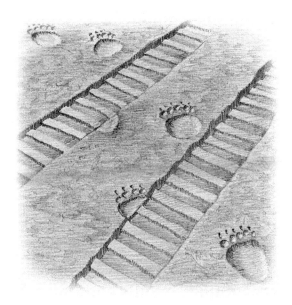

11
Caterpillar

It's about time you wake up!" Raven seemed to be saying when Daniel peeped out from under the tarp the next morning. The rain had stopped and Raven was cocking his head from side to side, opening and closing his beak. His neck feathers were puffed out and his round black eyes were full of curiosity.

Before Daniel had time to respond, Raven jerked his head around. With a loud shriek, he flew off the branch, and continued to shriek as he flew in the direction of the poachers. Daniel wasn't surprised when he heard the sound of machinery closing in moments later. He cautiously leaned out over the edge of the platform and surveyed the forest below. He waited, ready to pull back if they looked up in his direction. But he knew that eventually they would start up the hill to survey the big cedar, sizing it up as their next victim. And when they did, he would be discovered.

The two came driving up on an old beaten-up yellow Caterpillar. Its metallic tread shredded the earth and mowed down everything in its path. They drove along next to the giant they had felled and appraised their work. "That's a beaut' all right. Let's see if we can find another one that big," Daniel heard them say.

When would they notice the big cedar on the hill? Daniel began to tremble. But then Raven returned silently to his perch, and Daniel pulled himself together.

One of the poachers—the younger one—jumped off the Caterpillar and took off on foot in the opposite direction from where Daniel was perched. The older one started up his chainsaw and while he drove the Cat around, steering with one hand, cut everything in sight with the other. After little was left but the bigger trees, he scanned the hillside. Daniel ducked back behind the tree, but then he peeked out and watched the Cat switchback up the hill, forging a clear path of destruction.

Daniel thought, *This is it. When he sees me here...*

"Whadya think yer doin' up there, kid?" the man roared when he spied Daniel. "If ya don't get down fast, this tree's comin' down and you'll be with it!"

"No way. I won't come down until you stop logging this island!" At that moment, Raven took off with a "Quok! Quok!" that reverberated through the forest.

Then Daniel began to shake so uncontrollably that the platform vibrated. *Is he bluffing?* Daniel agonized. *Did I see a gun? Will he back off or...? Will I have the guts to call his bluff?*

Like so many vultures, doubts circled his mind. *Jeez, this must be crazy! Leonard said it was. But I just wouldn't give up on it.*

What if Leonard doesn't make it back in time? What if he doesn't come back at all—he did that once before!

Daniel's attention was drawn to hundreds of ravens darkening the sky overhead. They gathered even more numbers and started on a gradual descent, making a clatter so deafening that it drowned out even the sound of the Caterpillar and the chainsaw. His eyes followed them as they circled lower and lower until they were flying at the level of the platform and the wind whipped up by their beating wings forced him back against the tree. When they settled to the ground, Daniel was startled to find that the poacher had disappeared.

Then with a great flutter, they flew off into the forest.

All but one.

Raven had stayed back and returned to the branch near Daniel. Still shaking from the encounter with the poacher, Daniel was glad to see Raven sidle up close and take up where he had left off when the poachers came. He fluffed out the feathers on his head and made soft gurgling sounds that calmed Daniel down. When Raven took off and flew upward into the now blue and white patchwork sky, Daniel sat back on his platform with arms folded behind his head and watched Raven perform amazing aerial acrobatics. The big bird soared, rolled and dove, for at least an hour. By the time Raven flew off with a long, deep "quok," Daniel's body had stopped twitching every time he heard a sound from the forest below.

Daniel and Raven spent the next several days in each other's company. When the wind began to blow again and rain fell in sheets, Daniel was forced to stay holed up under the tarp. Raven joined him there for a portion of each day—

probably, Daniel speculated, whenever he wasn't searching for food. Daniel decided to try out Father's carving knife, the one Leonard had given him. Taking out the small curved knife from its deerskin case, he stroked the smooth wooden handle, darkened and oily from years of use, and then balanced the knife on the tips of his outstretched fingers. The knife must have felt like this to Father, he thought.

Picking up a cedar plank, left over from building the platform, he spoke out loud, "What do you think, Raven? Will you pose for a carving?"

He would carve a raven figure, like the ones he did at home. But now he had a model to pose for him.

He looked closely at Raven, with an eye to capturing his likeness. His glossy black feathers reminded him of Grandfather's story about how it was that Raven turned a pitch black. As he was imagining how he would go about carving Raven's features—his beak, his eye, his wing—tracing the shapes in his mind, he could almost hear Grandfather's voice:

"Raven was all white then. But no one could see that because darkness was all around. Well, you know Raven, he got tired of flying around in the dark, bumping into things, so he came up with a plan. He would turn himself into a baby— the great Chief of the Sky would think it was his grandchild. Danny, that was Raven's way of tricking the chief into letting him into the longhouse. When the baby cried for something to play with, he figured the chief, being a good grandfather, would give him the cedar box of sunlight.

"Well, that's just what happened. Raven waited until the chief walked away. Then he opened the box. Inside the box was another box. Then another. Raven was getting nervous. When he opened the smallest box, light came flooding out. A shiny yellow ball full of light rolled out. And just when the chief came running back to take it away, Raven turned himself back into a bird. He grabbed the yellow ball in his beak and flew up through the smokehole. It was the smoke that made his feathers black. When Raven was outside—you know Raven, sometimes he's clumsy—he dropped the ball on the ground. It broke into pieces. That's how we got the sun, the moon, and the stars."

When Daniel looked at Raven again, he pondered what made him different from the others. It was the V-shaped gap in the feathers of Raven's wing that set him apart. Daniel had noticed it when Raven was performing his aerial show, and he had wondered what kind of fierce skirmish left Raven marked like this. As if Raven knew what Daniel was thinking, he shook out his wings and Daniel got a glimpse of his V-shaped badge of valor. How would Daniel represent that badge in his carving?

He started by outlining the traditional shapes with the tip of his knife—large and small shapes that resembled O's, U's, V's and S's when looked at alone. But Daniel knew that when he put them all together, he would create a figure of a raven. He decided he would make a gap in the nested U's that the formed the wing—that's how he would capture Raven's spirit.

After outlining, he made little scooping cuts in the wood, releasing the sweet- pungent fragrance of cedar oil. He was determined to make all the cuts meet in clean angles, and he took pains to do the chiseling so finely that the knife marks were almost undetectable. Daniel had done many raven carvings before, but this one was feeling different, not just because he was spending more time and being more careful, but because he was really creating something. It felt "deep carved," as Grandfather would say.

Daniel thought about the last time he had carved a raven.

It was back on the streets of Seattle just weeks before, when everything started happening. When the eagle had looked him in the eye. It felt like a lifetime ago.

He had figured things were going to change.

And, boy, did they! Daniel concluded, turning his attention back to the task at hand.

Finally, he asked, "What do you think, Raven? Is it you?"

* * *

There were times during the next few days when Daniel missed Grandfather and Leonard terribly. Then Raven would sing melodious songs that would lull Daniel into a little nap. Daniel would let his carving knife drop to his lap and listen to Raven sing as he drifted off. Sometimes, Raven would come up to him, with his wing feathers puffed up so that he looked like he was wearing a billowing black cape. He would cock his head and look into Daniel's eyes. At those times, Daniel thought Raven really wanted to converse.

There were other times when Raven would yell; his cry would start at least a mile away and become earsplitting as he approached. But somehow Daniel knew not to be alarmed. He could tell the difference between this sound, which seemed just for fun, and the one when Raven had warned him of the poachers.

When Daniel thought about the poachers' return, which he figured was inevitable, he was nervous. But Raven was always there when Daniel needed to talk.

"What are we going to do when the poachers come back?"

Raven cocked his head.

"What if they have guns? We'll be sittin' ducks on this platform, won't we?"

Chuckling at the idea of talking to a raven about being a duck, Daniel squatted and started duck walking around the platform, flapping his elbows at his sides and quacking. When he looked back at Raven and saw him strutting along behind, Daniel rolled over on his back. The platform shook with his laughter.

Then he recalled the poachers. "Remember the first time they came? You called your friends in from every direction with that scream of yours."

Raven hopped up and down and clucked, his black eyes sparkling.

"OK, I've got a plan," Daniel said.

After paying close attention as Daniel relayed his plan, Raven fluttered his wings and clicked.

"So you agree, huh, Raven?"

Raven clicked again.

"I think we're really beginning to understand each other," Daniel said finally.

* * *

But it was Raven's second warning that made Daniel realize they had understood each other all along.

12
Rifle

Raven took off from his post with a scream. Daniel's body knew before his mind that someone was coming. Then he heard the gunshots. The vibration of the platform banging against the tree could almost have been mistaken for a woodpecker drilling for insects, but Daniel knew that the poachers wouldn't be fooled. He knew they were already headed for the hill where he was perched—like a bull's-eye—on the platform. He could picture them picking off every animal they ran across for their target practice. He thought of all the animals at the stream. He pictured the white bear fishing. He hoped against hope the poachers hadn't been there.

Questions raced through his mind. Were the poachers going to hunt him down? Or were they just going to try to scare him down from the tree?

Daniel began to chant over and over in a tremulous voice, "No matter what, I'm not leaving this tree." But no matter how determined he was, he couldn't stop himself from shaking.

The gunshots, chainsaw and Caterpillar together made a trio of nauseating sound, increasing in volume as each moment passed. Then an uproar in the sky drowned out the one on the ground. The throng of ravens had returned, called in from all directions by Raven's scream of distress, exactly according to plan. Even though Daniel felt as if his ears would burst, the ravens' return gave him hope. He looked up to see if he could find Raven. The light in the sky was totally eclipsed by the big black birds and he couldn't make out individuals, but he was confident Raven was there. Daniel looked down and saw the poachers in the lower forest. Both had rifles, the older was holding his weapon in one hand while steering the Caterpillar with the other. The younger one was firing his rifle indiscriminately with one hand while brandishing a buzzing chainsaw in the other.

Daniel was sure that their crazed behavior was meant for him. He knew it was time for him to carry out the next step of the plan—climb higher in the tree and find cover in the highest and largest branch. He could do it without ropes—all he had to do was make the leap across to another branch, lower down, but one that provided him a route upwards. From there he could climb limb to limb until he reached another major branch where he wouldn't be seen from the ground. The leap was long, but he had determined that it was possible.

Thinking back at the "discussion" he had had with Raven, he recalled the plan.

"I'll leap way over to that branch so I can climb higher. Can I do it, Raven?"

Raven had whistled in what Daniel took to be appreciation of the distance, but then clicked decisively—or so it seemed to Daniel.

"If they start sawing the cedar, I'll drop some salmon down on them and then you and your friends will swoop down to get it." Raven's head bobbed.

So far, Raven had kept his "word"—at his summons, ravens were now swarming overhead.

Drawing closer, the poachers kept up their shooting and sawing and hollering. Then they started their ascent up the hill, with only one purpose—to get Daniel out of the big cedar. Yes, if Daniel was to survive their assault, it was time to execute the next step of the plan and climb higher. When the poachers couldn't see him, they would think that he was cowering against the tree on the platform.

Do it now, he thought, before they come round the tree.

Grabbing the salmon skin and hooking it to his jeans, then stepping off the platform onto the limb, he felt the springy moss underfoot and doubted that it would give him enough stability to jump. So he dug his feet into the mossy cushion and crouched like a cougar.

He froze.

Staring at the chasm that separated him from his destination, doubts began to eat away at his nerve. *I've been talking to a bird!* he thought. *Raven can't understand me. The plan won't work—it's way too far for me to leap across.* His legs felt like stones. *I'm alone and there's no way out.*

Then, out of the corner of his eye, he realized that Raven had appeared at his side. As if leading the way, Raven flew from the branch where Daniel crouched to the other, where

Daniel needed to land. When Raven turned to look back at Daniel, Daniel's confidence returned.

He took the leap.

Daniel's moment in the air a hundred feet above the ground felt like a passage into another world. The commotion on the ground suddenly vaporized. He felt as if he were joining the throng of ravens above. For that moment, he was released from the earth.

Then he landed on the branch and had to dig his fingernails into the bark on the trunk of the cedar to keep himself from flying right over the edge.

No time for relief. Just start climbing faster than ever, he told himself. He grabbed hold of a limb and started up, banking on none of the limbs giving way. Just as he heard the Caterpillar come around the tree, he pulled himself up onto the huge branch he hoped would hide him from view and even shield him from bullets.

Daniel didn't dare look down. But he could hear the poachers close in on the tree. He heard one of them yell, "Hey, you little worm, we'll give you ten seconds to start down from the tree, or we're startin' to cut."

"Ten, nine, eight," they chanted, and started to laugh. "Hey, maybe he can't count!" the younger one mocked.

When the countdown reached one, the older one said, "OK, you asked for it!" and he started sawing the smaller spruce tree next to the big cedar—the same tree that Daniel had climbed for fun when he and Leonard were together. That seemed like ages ago.

When the older poacher sawed just to the point of no return, the younger one yelled, "Hey, Pa, stop! It'll go down right on the platform!"

"Had his chance!" the older one replied as he continued sawing with a vengeance.

Daniel didn't need to look to know what was happening. He heard the tree trunk being cut through by the whirring chainsaw. He could smell the gasoline fumes mixed with the spruce-scented sawdust. He could feel the vibration in the air as the spruce began to fall toward the big cedar and he could see the top of the spruce tree tearing some of the big cedar's branches off the trunk, just below where he stood. And, he could imagine the platform being ripped away from where it was secured, imagine his sleeping bag and pack, and his carving, dropping a hundred feet to the ground.

Daniel didn't need to look to know that the platform now dangled by a rope from the torn branch below.

He heard the older poacher exclaim, "He wasn't on the platform! Where the heck is that little no-good?" The poacher picked up his rifle and shot at random up into the tree.

The younger poacher didn't say anything.

"Well, let's get started, this is gonna take all day!" the older one said as he put down his rifle and picked up his chainsaw. He placed the long blade against the big cedar and pulled the cord to start it. The whirr of the chain rang through the forest with a metallic certainty.

Daniel felt the vibration and slumped to his knees. *They'll cut the tree and I'll go down with it*, he thought. Then he remembered the plan. He crept to the edge of the limb until he could see the poachers hundreds of feet below. Then he unhooked the salmon from his jeans and let it drop.

At that instant, the throng of ravens that had been circling overhead, shot past Daniel, as if they were going to dive deep into the earth. Hundreds of black birds surging by him. His pounding heart felt as if it would leap from his chest. Could it be that the plan was working?

On the ground the poachers looked up and saw salmon

and ravens raining down on them. They dropped their chainsaws and rifles and instinctively covered their eyes with their hands. Claws and beaks descended on them, tearing at whatever they found—fish or human, skin or flesh. Finally, with ravens swarming all around them, the poachers dropped to their knees and huddled in fetal positions, arms covering their heads. Curled up on the ground, the older one reached out and grabbed his rifle. He began to shoot randomly, still struggling to keep his head covered. When the shooting didn't scare the ravens off, the poachers crawled over to the Caterpillar. Dodging raven wings and claws, they started the engine and fled down the hill.

When Daniel could no longer hear the engine, he leaned over the branch to see what remained. At first he couldn't focus. Then he saw the platform dangling in the wind. Next he noticed the splintered ends of branches that had been severed by the falling spruce. On the forest floor, he was able to make out the chainsaws and the rifles. He saw his raven carving. Then he saw Raven himself—lying immobile on his back on the ground, wings spread out exposing his V-shaped badge.

Daniel lowered his head onto the bough. The moss absorbed his tears.

13
Totem Pole

As soon as he pulled himself up onto the branch where Daniel was stranded, Leonard began telling his brother the story of how they had apprehended the poachers at the shore.

Handing Daniel a bottle of water and a sandwich, he said, "Looks like you really scared them, Danny. I don't know how you did it, but they looked like they had seen a ghost. They were actually pretty easy to detain. They didn't have any guns and they just stood and stared at us when we jumped out of the boat."

While Leonard was telling the story, Daniel was imagining the parts Leonard might be leaving out. Like how nervous

Grandfather and Leonard must have been when they saw the two big men, tattered and scratched up, trying to make a hasty retreat from the island. And how scared they must have felt when the poachers refused to say they had seen Daniel—the younger one looking especially guilty when Daniel's name was mentioned. And how much dread Grandfather and Leonard must have had when they were hiking through the forest, seeing the carnage and destruction, not knowing what they'd find.

Daniel recalled how, when he had been awakened from a fitful sleep up in the tree by panicked voices shouting "Danny! Danny!" he knew it was Grandfather and Leonard. Before they could hear his reply, he guessed they had discovered the platform dangling from the branch and all the gear strewn on the ground.

But now, one thing he knew of one thing for sure—their relief at being back together.

"Grandfather's pretty proud of you, Danny."

Daniel leaned over the branch and waved at Grandfather, who looked small and frail, and was looking up at them. Daniel scanned the forest floor and saw that Raven's body was no longer there.

"What happened to the raven they shot, Leonard?" Daniel asked, trying to conceal the emotion that welled up inside of him when he thought of Raven.

"Grandfather picked him up and put him into his pack. He said he knew that you'd want to bury him. He said that he thought Raven had helped save your life, Danny."

Daniel composed himself for a few moments. "Not just mine, Leonard."

Then he stood up and took the climbing rope from Leonard's hand, cinched up the harness and started his descent down the big cedar. "Let's do some fishin' before we go home, OK, Leonard?"

* * *

"Grandfather!"

Grandfather beamed as Daniel hopped to the ground. As they bear hugged, he said, "You are a brave boy. You have a good story to tell, don't you, Danny?"

"Grandfather, before I tell you the story, I want to see Raven."

Grandfather carefully opened his pack and slowly slid Raven's rigid body onto the ground. Kneeling down, Daniel saw the caked blood on his breast where the bullet had entered his body. He remembered talking with Raven about their plan and how Raven had helped protect him from the poachers.

Daniel stroked the feathers on Raven's head and said, "Raven, I've thought about it and I'm going to carve a memorial pole for you back home. It'll be a tall cedar pole and it'll stand on the big rock at the shore. When people come to our village, they'll see you first—you'll be high up on the pole and your great carved beak will protect our home."

Imagining the pole he would carve as he talked about his adventures, he said, "Let's see, below Raven there'll be an eagle with her straight wings and keen eye, then the tasty crab. In the middle of the pole a whale will be leading us through the fog, and then below the whale, a seal will play. At the bottom, a mother wolf will look on as the white bear sits clasping the mighty salmon."

B.J. JOHNSON

Daniel looked up at Grandfather and asked, "Will you help me carve the pole, Grandfather?"

"No, Danny," he said holding out his gnarled hands, "these are no good anymore. You know Raven will play a trick on us if the pole isn't deep carved."

"But these hands are!" Leonard called from above, as he slid down the rope. "I'll help, Danny. It's time we worked together on a project."

"OK, Leonard, but I get to carve Raven," Daniel replied with a smile.

* * *

As Grandfather, Leonard and Daniel started their hike back to the boat, they heard a raven's "Quok! Quok!" fill the forest. When Daniel looked up and glimpsed a dark shape disappearing into the canopy, his body tingled with the same sensation he felt when he had made his leap high up in the big cedar. But in his mind he was already at home carving Raven's pole from another cedar.

END

AUTHOR'S NOTE

The Island of the Ghost Bear really exists. It is Princess Royal Island and you can find it by looking at a map of the west coast of British Columbia, among the myriad islands of the Inside Passage.

Are the friendly white bears of the island that "have never been hunted" still enjoying the clear, cold water of the island streams and the salmon that spawn there? At this writing, the answer is yes. Due to the tireless efforts of many people, the island has not been logged. But it takes constant work and vigilance by people in organizations like the Valhalla Wilderness Society to make sure that the island is protected from habitat destruction, not just poaching and clear-cut logging, but also over-fishing, development and industrial pollution, to name a few. Though the white bear seems special, all the bears on the coast of British Columbia are precious and deserve protection. As Daniel and Leonard saw, the bears' existence depends on their habitat—the temperate old growth rainforest—one of the earth's great treasures. Beautiful photos and fascinating information about the white bears is presented in Charles Russell's book, *Spirit Bear: Encounters with the White Bear of the Western Rainforest*.

Another very real treasure of the Northwest is the splendid artwork of the Northwest Coast Native peoples. Daniel and Leonard are, of course, fictional characters, and where they are from, Hannah Island, is also fictional. But their Northwest

Coast native culture (the book draws from three cultures, Tsimshian, Haida and Kwagiulth) is real and thriving. That wasn't always the way it was. At the end of the 19th and beginning of the 20th centuries, it was the policy of both the U.S. and Canadian governments that the Native Americans should abandon their beliefs and their cultural practices. So, potlatches were banned, children were sent to boarding schools where they were forbidden to dress in their traditional ways and forced to speak English, and totem poles were taken from where they proudly stood and placed in museums and private art collections. Many Native American artists in the Northwest, like Leonard in the story, have reclaimed their traditions and have started an artistic movement that is now recognized around the world. Their works meld the techniques of their ancestors with their own visions of the future.

The young woman in the story whose picture Daniel sees in the newspaper is a real person named Julia Butterfly Hill. She decided to spend as long as it would take sitting in a 1000-year old redwood tree she named Luna to stop a logging company from cutting it down. It took more than two years. Her book, *The Legacy of Luna,* is an account of her life in the tree. After her book was published, a vandal tried to destroy Luna by cutting it with a chainsaw. Even though the cut went through sixty percent of its eleven-foot diameter, the tree could be saved. A number of arborists and foresters kept it from falling in strong winds by installing steel braces above and below the cut. Some of the branches will atrophy but, with care, it may last another 1000 years.

SUGGESTED ADDITIONAL READING

Heinrich, Bernd. *Mind of the Raven: Investigations and Adventures with Wolf-Birds.* New York: Cliff Street Books, 1999.

Hill, Julia. *The Legacy of Luna: The Story of a Tree, a Woman and the Struggle to Save the Redwoods.* San Francisco: Harper, 2001.

Hoyt-Goldsmith, Diane. *Potlatch: A Tsimshian Celebration.* New York: Holiday House, 1997.

McAllister, Ian, and McAllister, Karen. *The Great Bear Rainforest: Canada's Forgotten Coast.* San Francisco: Sierra Club Books, 1997.

Reid, Bill, and Bringhurst, Robert. *The Raven Steals the Light.* Seattle: University of Washington Press, 2003.

Russell, Charles. *Spirit Bear: Encounters with the White Bear of the Western Rainforest.* Toronto: Key Porter Books Limited, 1994.

Stewart, Hilary. *Looking at Indian Art of the Northwest Coast.* Seattle: University of Washington Press, 1979.

Stewart, Hilary. *Looking at Totem Poles.* Seattle: University of Washington Press, 2003.